Love

in the Sand
and the Snow

DEE DISHEAU

Order this book online at www.trafford.com
or email orders@trafford.com

Most Trafford titles are also available at major online book retailers.

Print information available on the last page.

ISBN: 978-1-4907-2676-2 (sc)
ISBN: 978-1-4907-2675-5 (e)

Trafford rev.   07/07/2015

Trafford
PUBLISHING®   www.trafford.com
North America & international
toll-free: 1 888 232 4444 (USA & Canada)
fax: 812 355 4082

To my daughter

CONTENTS

CHAPTER ONE

Ashton Lakes Estate. What a stroke of luck to have stumbled upon it. And right in the middle of the affable city of Sarasota too. It was too good to be true, country in the city so to speak. Low-rise buildings lent an air of dignity to the residents lucky enough to live there. Small spring-fed lakes formed a magic around which the condos had been constructed. Built over a decade ago on a few square acres of land, the estates were barely eight minutes from Siesta Key which boasted the world's purest sand and the most breathtaking sunsets on earth.

Leaving the bustling city of Toronto, Canada's claim to metropolianity, only a week before, Tanya had been desperate to get away from it all. She still hurt deeply every day, all day long, when she thought of Brad and his cruel goodbye. It had been so impersonal and so final. True, for quite some time things between them had been strained and unfulfilling, but because of the time they had invested in their relationship, both were reluctant to let go. As a result their loving marathon had continued. But finally things had gotten so predictable that the oomph, that lovers should feel, had slowly seeped away, leaving Tanya stuck with one big stumbling block, that of considering love versus habit. To her they were synonymous. She couldn't separate one from the other and it was driving her crazy. She had tried numerous times to discuss her concerns with Brad but he seemed okay with things just as they were. Most of the time that was! Nevertheless, as a result of her begging, he had agreed to seeking out a counselor and complying with his suggestions so as to give Tanya peace of mind. This meant putting their wedding plans on hold as well as taking separate vacations.

CHAPTER TWO

Morning came early for Tanya. On the heels of an especially restless night, she had gotten out of bed, made coffee, and carried it to the patio where she settled into a comfortable over stuffed chair. From this vantage point she prepared to greet the sunrise and further wallow in her personal sea of misery. For the hundredth time she rehashed her relationship with Brad and wondered where they went wrong. Where had she gone wrong? And what on earth had caused his about face concerning their game plan. She wondered if it was still possible to put love back on the agenda.

Tanya's thoughts tumbled over one another when she recalled the newness of their love. Back then the whole world had seemed newly washed and newly dressed. It had all seemed so long ago. It was almost like the high school hangover, but way back then they'd been able to turn the mundane into the magical. Maybe their hunger for security had been too great and in the end it had been their undoing.

Tanya continued to sit as still as a statue, eyes closed tight, listening to a distant voice far in the back of her mind. This voice was telling her that everything was going to be okay. It assured her that they would meet the challenge that love laid down. Her brow furrowed as her reverie was disturbed by the gradual, then frantic, dance of the white egrets that by now ringed the lake. At first there was just a few, but soon dozens and dozens appeared, as they cavorted near the edge of the water, squawking and fanning the air with their flailing wings. Each fought to protect its established fishing strip. The sun rose quickly and with the sunrise the pond life, so active in the night time, became placid, then finally still. Hours would pass before Tanya left her chair, still no closer to solving her Brad dilemma than she had been since receiving his awful fax.

By noon the sun was already relentless as Tanya struggled to tug her scanty mauve bikini up over her perspiring body. Carefully she packed her tote bag in preparation for her initial visit to the pool. Towel, thongs, and sunshades were carefully selected to ensure colour coordination. This would be her first visit to the pool and even a broken heart was no excuse for not looking one's best. When we look good, we feel good, Tanya reminded herself. Funny how such a personal principle could present itself at a time like this. The heart is breaking but colour coordination rules supreme.

Tanya ventured out into the glare of the sunshine and followed the signs indicating the location of the pool. She paused as she rounded the corner of the club house she was surprised to discover that the pool was Olympic-sized. Olympic-sized and completely uninhabited! Surrounding it were dozens of comfortable chairs and, off to the left, a shuffle-board beckoned players. Beautiful flowering shrubs and tall graceful palms were interwoven throughout the entire area. Two more majestic fountains competed in their effort to shoot water high into the air before it broke and ceremoniously entered the lake in preparation for repeating the continuous pattern.

Just as Tanya was pondering why the pool was uninhabited on such a stifling hot day, she was startled by a slight movement straight ahead of where she stood. Blending into the serenity around him lay a handsome male on a comfortable white lounger. Tanya wondered how long he had been watching her. He certainly made no effort to hide his blatant interest as he appraised her from head to toe and back again. Suddenly, Tanya felt uncomfortable in fact she found the situation intrusive and unsettling. It was a complication Tanya had not counted on.

The stranger was handsome and she guessed him to be somewhere in his late twenties or early thirties. It was hard to tell because of his tousled hair and rugged features. Titanium white teeth made a striking contrast to his darkened skin. Skin that dark could only be the result of sunshine mayhem, so he must be Floridian. Muscles rippled over his ribs like an old-fashioned washboard and his stomach was hard and flat. He certainly had all the ingredients of a modern macho. No doubt, he was an egotistical specimen to boot. Probably one who spent his time at the beach spinning his dreams on the glory of seduction. But all of it was wasted on Tanya. She was too preoccupied with a love gone wrong.

"I'm glad you came to share the pool with me", said the stranger.

Tanya ignored him as she pretended to study the surroundings.

"It's a shame to let it go to waste on such a gorgeous day", he continued.

Tanya was perplexed. True, the pool was for everyone. But her privacy was her own and this brash stranger had no right to invade her personal space. In Toronto one didn't strike up a conversation with virtual strangers. Maybe Sarasota was different.

"How long are you staying here?" he persisted.

"Just a few weeks", Tanya surprised herself by answering. He had caught her completely unaware.

"That's great. We can spend some time together. I rent the same condo year after year. Seems like home to me now".

Tanya found his brashness alarming. She wasn't in the mood for such flirtatious behaviour. Nor was she flattered or impressed by his unmasked interest. There was only room for one man in her thoughts. That man was Brad. She had no intention of being caught up in this handsome stranger's friendly web. She preferred to be alone with her thoughts of Brad, even if the thoughts were steeped in misery.

Deliberately choosing a comfortable lounge chair, as far away from the over-friendly stranger as she could get, Tanya spread out her thirsty towel before liberally applying sunscreen, and positioned herself on the chair. She coaxed the sun to toast her milky-white Canadian skin, as she turned once more to the dilemma of Brad.

"Suppose to be hot all week", said the lounge from the end of the pool. Tanya decided not to answer. She would refuse to acknowledge his presence. Maybe he'd take the hint and go away. She sat with her eyes closed. Thinking. Hurting. Wanting to fly home. Fix things. Get life back on track.

The warm rays riveted Tanya's body to the chair. Perspiration ran down the small of her back. She desperately wanted to wipe it away and move to a more comfortable position but how could she do it without drawing attention to herself? She wished she had positioned herself facing away from the bronzed sun lover. But, it was too late for that also as he was directly in her line of vision, and she, in his. The best she could hope for was that he would soon get his quota of sun and leave. There was nothing to do but bide her time and pray for his departure.

Tanya closed her eyes once more, and continued to torture herself with thoughts of Brad and her over-reaction to the ugly fax. She focused upon his warm earnest look of concern as they had futilely discussed the pros and cons of marriage. Sex was never an option for discussion, even though; it had been the biggest problem of all. Brad considered himself a healthy young male with a normal sex drive and all the expectancies that went with it. Tanya, on the other hand, thought it took the sheen off their affair, maybe even jaded it a bit. She had been determined to suffocate Brad's advances, determined to hold out for sex within the confines of marriage. Their codes were different but their desires were the same. Brad simply didn't possess the patience that she did and now it seemed that he had given up. He had come to consider their love a juvenile charade which he no longer wished to be part of. Or perhaps the waiting game, besides dousing his emotional fires, had taken a serious toll on his patience. Whatever it was, she was here and he was there.

Sven spread his legs wide, hooked his heels into the vinyl cross straps of the lounger, and anchored his book on his up-bent knees. This arrangement served as a decoy for the furtive looks he cast in Tanya's direction. He liked what he saw. A beautiful statue, eyes closed, drinking in the golden rays. In between glances, Sven was methodically planning his strategy. It was during one of his clandestine glances that, quite by chance, he caught Tanya looking back. As their eyes locked, Tanya's face flushed red. It was not the heat of the day, or long exposure to the strong sunshine, but sheer embarrassment of the moment. She was mortified at being caught in such a covert act. A sudden feeling of guilt washed over her. In some perverse sense, despite all that had happened, it made her feel unfaithful to Brad. Well! She'd fix that. After delivering Sven her best withering glance, she awkwardly scooped up her towel and pool apparel and took her reddened face to the safety of the condo.

Once again, installed in her favourite chair, quietly sipping a tall, cool, glass of fresh-squeezed Florida sunshine, she returned to her cherished world of Brad. Had they been too hasty in parting? Would they ever reach a mutual level of agreement? Had she made too much fuss about the hastily sent fax? Around and round the unanswered questions went, churning through her mind, painful memories which pathetically needed answers. Tanya had to admit to herself that the acute pain of the last two days had somewhat diminished. But now, there was numbness in its wake. Which was preferable? Tanya really couldn't tell. Love and pain. Pain and love. Maybe love was pain. But her pain was always Brad-driven.

Maybe she should just consider their time spent together a cancelled cheque and move on. But where could she get the strength to do so? Tanya found herself frantic to outdistance the memories of Brad, memories that came unbidden, night and day, transparent and voiceless. Tanya sat for hours barely moving. But she wasn't wasting time. Her thinking was paying off. Her mind was tumbling facts, causes, and effects around and around. Things were no longer so lopsided, not as all-consuming and crippling as they had been a night or two ago.

Tanya smiled a knowing smile. Her mood was changing. She needed time. Now she realized the value of that time. For the first time since she had received the fax, Tanya understood that she had to take charge of her emotions and herself. This was imperative if she were to make a difference. She was ready to take that challenge now and she knew exactly what she had to do.

CHAPTER THREE

Brad felt exhilarated as the cold blast of winter filled his lungs. He felt as if he had been born for a life on the slopes. This higher purpose brought with it a super-special feeling, a feeling he had been experiencing since the tender age of five. It had been about that time that he had set his hopes on one day becoming a professional skier, or at the very least, a ski instructor. Anything concerning skiing would do. But his domineering mother had plans for him and had, slowly but surely, squashed his baby dream by directing him to the safer and more conventional world of computer study.

It had been a long drawn out struggle, but in the end, Brad had capitulated to his mother's wish and achieved the status of computer analyst. The achievement had been hollow; leaving him cloaked with a feeling of non-fulfillment. Yet today, the feeling of his mother's early interference kept him from fully enjoying his love of the slopes. His yearly ski trip was like getting a drink from his childhood well, and by drawing on his early ski experience, he was able to enjoy the challenge of slaloms and the mutual camaraderie of seasoned fellow skiers.

On this particular day, despite the fact that the weather was sunny and the ski conditions perfect, Brad had not performed with his usual acumen. The nighttime hours had been perforated by troubled dreams in which Tanya had persistently tripped throughout the whole night. His dreams were ambushed by visions of their perfect long lost love. Over coffee, just that morning, he had once again tried to figure out why it had been so hard to come to terms with Tanya. Perhaps both had failed to realize that rarely two people bring the same expectancies to a relationship. Too often, he and Tanya had been at cross-purposes. Tanya was a jealous person. She really thought that jealousy constituted love. As far as Brad was concerned, she couldn't have been more wrong. He considered her outlook, not only adolescent, but a total waste of time. Whatever the reason, it was obvious that they could not come to terms. This stalemate had ultimately ordered the execution of their love.

Brad had always felt that every adult life holds one compelling passion and his passion had been Tanya. The mistake he had made was in believing that she felt the same. Their compulsion for each other ran deep and the spectrum they embraced, ecstasy at one end, dashed hopes at the other, had been largely responsible for Brad's childish over-reaction. God! How he wished he could just turn back the clock and recall the stupid fax he had so unthinkingly sent off. He couldn't even hold out an apology because he had no idea where Tanya was. Florida was a big place. It would be like looking for a needle in a haystack. To make matters worse, Tanya's sister, Alicia, flatly refused to divulge even her phone number. So here Brad was. Stuck! Drowning, in recrimination and misgivings! Self-pity, helplessness, and panic braided into his nemesis of life. And he felt completely helpless in reengineering it.

Brad's mind wandered back to the first time his parents had taken him with them on a ski trip to Vermont, Mt. Stowe to be exact. His childish eyes had marvelled at the voluptuous snow-covered mountain crests rising out of the quaintness of the outlying villages. The rusticity of the rambling cedar inns had stuck in his mind. He mentally shivered when he recalled his first taste of the exquisite cheeses and the pure maple sugar for which Vermont is famous. These childhood experiences had taken root and had grown with each passing year, making skiing not just fun, but an integral part of his adult existence.

Later in the evening, alone with his cognac and a world of pain, sitting in a secluded corner of the ski lodge, thoughts concerning Tanya tortured his mind. He re-lived the first time he had invited Tanya tot the slopes. Although she had already skied on a few occasions, she made it abundantly clear that she didn't share his all-consuming passion for the sport. Perhaps she had been intimidated by his expertise and the unfair expectancies that she thought went with the territory. Perhaps he had expected too much, too fast. Whatever the reason, she had stopped early during the last few days, finally refusing to participate at all. Tanya much preferred to curl up with a book, before the cozy fireplace in the main lounge.

Tanya had also declined Brad's generous offer of skiing lessons. She didn't feel the need to improve her basic skills. She was happy with things just as they were, with the exception of sharing Brad with all the other skiers. Their special connectedness caused her to feel left out and pushed aside. Why couldn't Brad be content with just the two of them? Wasn't she enough for him? If not, why not? On the other hand, Brad hadn't been able to understand her refusal to hone her basic skills, which would allow both of them to enjoy the challenge of the higher slopes and maybe even develop a better relationship with other skiers of his caliber.

11

Tanya held her ground, throwing roadblock after roadblock into his plans, until finally her excuses caused Brad to become impatient, and eventually, to question the certainty he once felt about their relationship. Of course, he loved Tanya deeply but he wished she'd just grow up! Her fits of jealousy were really getting to him lately. It seemed that he was spending more time consoling her than he was having fun.

Brad couldn't believe how things in his life had shifted. Just a few short months ago, he had felt secure, and despite their differences, thought solutions were possible. He had always been quick to consider Tanya's positive points. She was beautiful, had a promising profession, and came from a stayed-married background. All were ideal ingredients for a wife. But he had to admit that skiing wasn't the only bugbear. Other factors had come into play as well. Her anemic approach to understanding his feelings was a big one. Another hurdle was her jealousy. Although completely unfounded, it was this unfair way of thinking that had caused even his faithfulness to come under fire. Her childish jealousy and her constant demand on his time were real downsides

Intimacy had ultimately become the biggest stumbling block. Brad was well beyond adolescence and felt insulted by having to relieve his sexual pressure at home, alone in the privacy of his bathroom, after an evening of heavy petting, followed by Tanya's standard refusal of sex. It was a refusal that he had come to expect, but never to accept. After all, they were engaged. Living in the nineties for god's sake!

Somewhere along the line, Brad had decided that the sexual sacrifice was just too problematic. Not that he wasn't used to sacrifice! His mother had seen to that a long time ago when he had been forced to sacrifice his ideal ski dream and replace it with computer studies. He had never come to terms with his mother's selfish demand. Her peace of mind was not the only consideration as far as he was concerned. She had forced him to cocoon himself in the safety net of computer analysis, something safe that he could always count on. Same old story! His mother had never let up. It had been easier to cave into her wishes than to listen to her. She had been a single mother who had sacrificed to give him all the things she, herself, had never had. And she never let him forget it.

The negative thoughts concerning Tanya, and his mother, eventually ganged up on Brad. The familiar depression and the lack of self-assurance partnered up all too often lately. Through his cobwebs of thought, he could hear the raucous dart game in progress all around him. Even the noisy hoots of his fellow skiers were not enough to elevate his spirits. Like so many times before, Brad rolled up his unhappy thoughts, tucked them away, and turned in early. He hoped that tomorrow would be a better day. Love was supposed to make you feel good, not sorry for shredded wasted years, he thought, as he pulled the heavy woolen blanket up over his head to shut out the happy sounds from down the hall.

CHAPTER FOUR

Brad was up early, happy to greet a day airbrushed by softly falling snow and intervals of weak sunshine. Quite a brisk wind had blown up over night and was making itself felt as Brad neared the top of Mt. Stowe. He paused, drinking in the magnificent view of the splendid sight below. His past and present meshed as he relished the familiar scene. He never tired of this moment no matter how many times he had lived it. The cozy flat-roofed inns and the tiny chalets, interspersed between the lazy winding roads and inviting trails, was the most beautiful sight on earth as far as Brad was concerned. As usual, Brad's gaze was drawn back to the first part of the decent which he had mastered so long ago. He smiled as he thought of how many times he had effortlessly done this particular run.

Brad stared at the inviting descent, which dropped sharply before immediately twisting and turning into serpentine hairpin curves. It certainly wasn't a trail for novices, Brad proudly thought to himself, as he made last minute adjustments to his goggles and gloves before pushing off. Smoothly he executed the challenges that the first part of the trail offered and was pleasantly surprised, as he approached the second part, to notice that the wind had quieted to little more than a breeze. It would certainly make for a more enjoyable run. He had the mountain almost entirely to himself, as only a few other skiers glided along the smooth surface, their speed curtailed by the unexpected, intermittent, gusts of gritty snow and the sudden invisibility they caused.

Despite an excellent start, midway down the second part of the descent, Brad felt his ski loosen, then completely dislodge. This might have spelled disaster for a less experienced skier but excellent maneuverability, born from years of practice, managed to keep Brad upright and under control. Quickly, he moved off the side of the run, in order to assess the damage to his left ski binding. As he wrestled with the stubborn buckle, a fellow skier zoomed around the hairpin curve, flying by so closely that Brad found himself covered by the feathery plume of her wake. At least, he thought it was a 'she', but he had barely managed to catch a glance of her zooming figure through the shower of snow. She seemed vaguely familiar, but maybe it was just his imagination playing tricks on him. Every skier on the slopes had a same-ness, created by their sleek suits, balaclavas, and goggles. Little did Brad know that this single close encounter was to set the stage for a future face-to-face meeting. Neither could he have known that the remainder of his holiday was about to be seriously enhanced.

Brad brushed the snow off his hair and out of his eyes and once more got back to the business of the loosened ski. Aside from the inconvenience of the broken strap, as well as the close call of the zooming female skier, Brad considered his day on Mt. Stowe to be quite satisfactory. He trudged steadily downhill toward the waiting ski patrol and, by the time he entered the chalet, there was a spring in his step. He was eager to seek out fellow ski-lovers. Part of the overall joy of skiing came from sharing the après-ski drinks and joining in the friendly banter that all skiers are noted for. It is a camaraderie born of special people. This evening, skiers of varying age and ability filled the homey, if somewhat musty, lodge. Voices grew louder with each addition of ski team and, of course, their vainglorious trainers. Recreational skiers, although fewer in numbers, were also present. Likewise, the families that every weekend brought joined the group.

Small talk, good-natured cajoling, and compliments concerning individual achievements, punctuated the family atmosphere. Being recognized as a superb skier, Brad looked forward to the lauds that never failed to come his way. At this particular low ebb of his life, Brad needed and welcomed the positive input. Maybe it would serve to boost his personal slump concerning Tanya. Skiing was like balm to his wounded ego and he was egotistical enough to consider himself, not only one of the best skiers, but THE very best.

A friendly fire crackled in the great hearth causing the smell of pine to permeate the air. Brightly coloured sweaters were the trademark of all the patrons. Some were old favourites, some were stylish, while others were just plain comfortable. And Brad was right there among them. Carefully, he made his way through the noisy crowd, seeking out someone, anyone, to talk to. As he carefully nudged through the large pub area, his eyes took in the archway leading to the main dining room. He drank in the warmth provided by the beamed ceiling, and the musty stuccoed walls. This was home to him. He belonged here. He felt secure and happy to be part of such a familiar ski family.

Tantalizing aromas were being emitted from the enormous kitchen, just off to the left. A huge dining room table, designed to accommodate dozens of patrons in a single setting, sat squarely in the center of the room. Before long, loud chimes would announce the evening meal. Brad could hardly wait. Being a bachelor had its drawbacks and cooking was definitely high on Brad's drawback list. In fact, Brad sometimes wondered which ranked higher, his love of home cooking or his passion for skiing. One, or both, provided the magnet which drew him back to the lodge year after year. Meats, exotic sauces, vegetables and potatoes served in every imaginable form vied for space on the great wooden table. Brad had already looked forward to a treat of chocolat gateau and crème Brule to round off his perfect evening dinner. A meal like that was pretty hard to beat by anybody's standards. With so much food to choose from, Brad sometimes had a hard time making up his mind. As usual, he would pass up the glistening fresh fruit, because he could get that any day he wanted it. The combination of skiing and eating bordered on erotic. Only one other combination even came close, and that was exotic food and solid sex. The very thought of it plunged him back into a somber mood.

As Brad waited for dinner, he thought of likely never getting the chance to entice Tanya into sharing his views. Because of her puritan outlook, he had been forced to sacrifice his need for a healthy sexual release which, in turn, had created havoc with his emotional well-being. No doubt it had also been largely responsible for the trial separation and his unorthodox 'goodbye'. He again chastised himself for sending the fax. How could he have been so stupid?

"Good effort today!" Brad looked up in surprise, before pivoting all the way around to see who was addressing either his skiing ability or lack of it. He knew he was an excellent skier, so maybe it was just a clumsy attempt by a fellow skier to be facetious. Brad found himself staring into a pair of the dancingest green eyes he had ever seen. Eyes at home in a porcelain white face, framed by shoulder-length auburn hair. Ultra-white teeth enhanced her sassy smile. Brad appraised her quickly, noticing that her five and a half foot frame was curvaceous and well-proportioned. Her breasts were firm and taut and her hips knew exactly where to quit. At first, the upturned face before him seemed to radiate a childlike exuberance but, on closer study, the eyes belied the wisdom of an experienced woman. The coexistence of the girl-woman qualities made for an interesting study, but it was the eyes that piqued Brad's interest. He had seen those eyes before. But where? When? He felt that he knew her but just couldn't dredge up the connection.

"Good effort!" the woman stated for the second time. "Skiing is second nature to me. I don't need to make an effort", Brad firmly stated. "Oh, no! Not the skiing!" I'm referring to keeping your ski on and remaining vertical!" Recognition suddenly dawned on Brad. Standing before him was the skier who had sprayed him on the hairpin curve as he wrestled with the stubborn strap of he ski binding. He studied her closely. She had to be the skier, who had fanned out the wide white plume of snow, on her wild descent to the bottom of the run.

"Hope I didn't offend you. Or any part of your male assemblage! If I did, I'm sorry. Just join me for a drink and I'll kiss it better", she challenged, rocking sassily from side to side. Brad suddenly felt edgy, caught off guard by the stranger's cockiness, but considered her invitation a better alternative than sitting alone, brooding over Tanya.

"Name's Mitch", she offered, hitching one hip up on the nearest barstool as she patted the one beside her. "I'm Brad". "I thought so. I knew I had met you before. Go to Lawrence High?" "Yeah. As a matter of fact, I did." "Me too! I was in your class. Two rows behind you, one seat over. Michelle Dorey!" Brad's jaw dropped in astonishment. This brash creature couldn't be the avid bookworm from grade eleven! Brad grudgingly accepted her invitation, by slipping onto the stool beside her.

Over the span of two drinks he learned that Mitch, formerly Michelle, had a four-year-old son, product of a ski instructor husband, who had tragically died in an avalanche when their son was barely eighteen months of age. As they talked, Brad could tell that the passage of time had not yet been great enough to allow Mitch to forget. Tears filled her beautiful eyes as she recalled the painful past. Brad reached for her hand and gently squeezed it as a gesture of compassion. Mitch had always been quick to compose herself and tonight would be no different. Quickly she cleared her throat and whispered, "After the shock wore off, I found myself left with responsibility of raising my son and saddled with the legacy my husband left—an absolute love of skiing!"

Enough about me! Now, what about you? Brad still held onto her hand far longer than was necessary, caressing the bumps of her knuckles with his index finger. "My story is humdrum compared to yours", Brad stated. "Let's go to the dining room before all the food is gone".

Over dinner Brad relaxed and talked easily about his job, and of course, his passion for skiing. When he reached the part about his engagement to, then ultimately the breakup with, Tanya his voice almost broke. He finished in a strident monotone, as he described in detail the trial separation. Haltingly, he included the hastily sent fax. By the time his monologue ended, he was lost in thought, talking only to himself. Now it was Mitch's turn to squeeze his hand, but instead, she opted for hugging him close to her shapely bosom.

Gradually, Mitch and Brad, the sad recipients of lost loves, steered their conversation to safer grounds and a more positive course—their mutual addiction to the slopes. The dining room had emptied of its patrons, dishes had been cleared away, and still Brad and Mitch, heads bowed together, continued their long serious conversation. "I'm not going to sit here and pretend I'm some kind of saint", Mitch stated, I'm just a single young woman looking for a special kinda guy to help set my world straight. Maybe even provide that soft place to fall." Brad gave no indication that he either heard, or appreciated, what Mitch was working toward.

Long silences ensued as Brad toyed with his cold coffee, and Mitch prolonged her espresso, one sip at a time. Both knew they were warding off the inevitability of facing an empty room and a long lonely night. But mornings in the lodge came early, so Mitch slowly folded her napkin and stood up. Brad followed her lead, walking a few steps behind her as they left the dining salon and entered the narrow dim hallway leading to the rustic sleeping quarters.

Brad never took his eyes off the girl before him as he walked trance-like down the hall. Mitch was tall and slim, her body feminine, yet sinewy, from years on the slopes. Long legs led up to barely flaring hips. Tonight her tiny waist was encircled by a sequined belt, which winked and twinkled with each purposeful stride. A cable knit sweater made from baby-fine angora, had been purposely been chosen to compliment the green of her eyes. Obviously, the girl before him had left nothing up to chance. Brad, so intent on the study before him, almost collided with her firm up-turned behind when she suddenly stooped to unlock her bedroom door. "I'm sorry!" Brad apologized, "I didn't expect that sudden stop. You should signal!" "Weren't you watching?" Mitch challenged. "That's the trouble. I was watching too closely." "Wanna come in for a nightcap?" Mitch cooed. Brad met her imploring emerald eyes, then to ease the tension of his refusal, quipped, "Since we've talked most of the night away, I think we'll need the rest of it to catch a few winks before our 8 a.m. run".

Brad couldn't help but notice Mitch's obvious disappointment, nor did he miss the wanton desire that shone like a beacon as she softly mouthed "g'nite" and slipped inside. Her intent was obvious and in other given circumstances, Brad would have been more than happy to acquiesce. But that this point in time, he wasn't ready to share in her agenda. Things were moving too fast. He was still battling the gain, then loss, of love. He was trying in vain to let time become a salve to his badly bruised ego.

Alone, in his bed Brad tossed and turned. His mind took turns battling the demons of Tanya and the loss of her love. Mitch's intangible promise of sexual satisfaction had also squirreled its way into a tiny recess of his mind. Squeezed between his devotion to Tanya and his obligation to himself, Brad wrestled with what direction he should take. He knew full well that he could not survive on memories alone. He needed new discoveries, and opportunities for making use of those discoveries. Perhaps tonight had been one of those opportunities and he had turned it down. A paradoxical mixture of 'shoulds' and 'should nots' pervaded his senses, as he finally drifted off into an uneasy sleep.

CHAPTER FIVE

The day dawned early and hot, a Floridian pattern consistent for this time of year. Despite her broken heart, Tanya found herself brooding less and less over Brad as the lazy days rolled one into another. And it helped that she'd been lucky enough to have befriended an interesting couple who had taken her under their wings and never failed to include her in their various social activities. Bob and Yvonne were older than Tanya and had travelled extensively over their years together.

Tanya loved to listen to their interesting accounts of trips to exotic places around the world. Besides that, they had a penchant for living each day to the fullest. Vonne, as she preferred to be called, was the envy of all her female friends. Her natural beauty, her lively nature, and, last but not least, her size four figure, were all ingredients for social success and good times. Bob complimented Vonne and her lifestyle, in that his financial successes and his desire to please, allowed him to plan and carry out their travel pursuits. Each had been married before and each had grown children. They quickly pointed out, to all who would listen, how lucky they felt to have met and to have a second chance. They considered themselves lucky to have time to spin dreams of their very own.

Being hell-bent on not wasting one precious moment, and always looking for a party, it was only natural that Vonne would eventually meet up with, and develop a passing relationship with Sven, the sun god, who seemingly reserved the large white lounge at the end of the pool. Sven loved being poolside, and besides, it was a strategic position for interacting with everyone coming and going to the Ashton Lakes community centre.

Since their initial meeting, Tanya had purposely avoided Sven. She found his unbridled interest and over-friendly gestures disconcerting. Notwithstanding that she now felt better about life in general, it was simply more than she wished to deal with at this particular point in time.

Every alternative Wednesday was the day set aside for special activities in the pool area. Today a potluck luncheon was planned. This would be followed by a rousing afternoon of fun and games. Tanya had had no intention of going but, at Vonne's persistence, she found herself heading for the pool, armed with her contribution of salmon pate and rice crackers.

The previous evening had dragged. The loneliness had been unbearable, provoking memory pains that were heightened by the dull ache of Brad's absence. She was counting on this luncheon to provide a much-needed diversion. Tanya hungered for a distraction from her 'Brad' thoughts. Logic told her that it was up to herself to create happiness in her very unhappy world.

By the time Tanya arrived at poolside, many guests were already there and a party mode permeated the atmosphere. Naturally, Vonne was front and center. "Over here! Over here,

Tanya", she shouted. Heading toward the other side of the pool, Tanya noticed an empty chair that had been saved beside Bob and Vonne. She inhaled nervously when she noticed that the suntanned god she had met on her initial visit to the pool was one of the noisy intimate revellers. Just what I need, she thought, to be in the company of the pompous male who had majored in obnoxious behaviour.

"Tanya, meet Sven", bubbled Vonne. "We've met", murmured Tanya, immediately on guard and determined to combat the naked interest he seemed hell-bent on displaying. Sven showed no signs of having been previously snubbed. Instead, he made a great show of welcoming Tanya into the group. It crossed Tanya's mind that maybe she had blown their first chance meeting out of proportion. Or could it be that he was using this lucky break to increase his chance at intimacy with what he considered to be an elusive Canadian beauty? Tanya wasn't sure but she was on guard. After all, parties could be dangerous places, she reminded herself. She had seen it all before, where drinks led to more drinks, and those drinks, in turn, led to racy conversations with every word and every gesture designed to promote ultimate orgiastic outcomes. Well! She'd have none of that. She was just here to fill time, not start something she had no intention of finishing.

Once the awkwardness of the introduction had worn off, Tanya, despite a resolution to diet properly, found her reserve slipping away as she readily accepted the drinks and little tidbits that Sven held out. As the afternoon progressed, Tanya eagerly joined in the rowdy game of water tennis and the shuffle board contests, always as Sven's partner of course. Maybe she had misread his earlier intentions, she told herself. Perhaps he wasn't the moral terrorist she had thought him to be after all. One thing she knew for sure was that the combination of the hot Florida sunshine and the magnetism of Sven created a wonderful sensory diversion from her troubles, especially in contrast to Brad and the dull Toronto atmosphere that now seemed so far behind her.

After several hours of food and frolic, things took on a more subdued air and, tired and overdue for their usual afternoon siestas, the luncheon crowd noisily dispersed. Showers and shuteye in the cool of their condos were absolute necessities before revving up for the five-o-clock happy hour. Even Tanya herself felt pleasantly exhausted. No. Exhausted was not the word. She felt relaxed. It was the kind of relaxation she had not felt since arriving in Florida. Maybe I'm coming to grips with my problems after all, thought Tanya. She actually smiled as she leisurely strolled back to her condo.

No sooner had Tanya closed her condo door behind her, than the phone rang. Must be a wrong number. Nobody but her sister even knew where she was. "Let's skip the cocktail hour and whip out for some real junk food later on", Sven's voice boomed in her ear. "I'll think about it ", Tanya stammered before quickly hanging up. On second thought, Tanya panicked. Sven had caught her completely off guard. It was one thing to frolic all afternoon with a crowd at the pool, but quite another to make a move like this. How presumptuous can a casual acquaintance get? The shrill ring of the phone once more shattered her thoughts. "Did we get cut off or something? I'll pick you up about six!" he continued, giving her no time to refuse or to find an excuse for not going along with his spur-of-the-moment plans. Tanya stared at the humming phone in her hand. Sven had already hung up and she couldn't even call him back. Well! Here was a man who really needed a lesson. How on earth could anyone be so presumptuous? He certainly was forward. And badly lacking in control—self-control, that is!

After selecting and discarding three casual outfits, Tanya, despite scolding herself for being foolish, was ready when the doorbell rang on the dot of six. Sven chatted easily on the way to the car, treating this date as just a normal everyday occurrence. But while Sven was handling things in an ultra-casual manner, Tanya was trying to cope with a heart that was beating as rapidly as if it was her very first teenage date. She made excuses for herself by thinking that it was no big deal really, and besides, hadn't she promised her self-esteem a brand new makeover? Yes. She was due. She had suffered a lot over the last two vicious weeks. She was tired of crying over her lack of romance, her lack of happiness, her lack of a shoulder to cry on. Every woman carries within her a fantasy of how life should be and she was no different. That's what she had done with Brad and it hadn't worked out. But she'd just have to get over it. Get on with living as painful as it might be. Maybe tonight, if she was lucky, she could re-route her misery if only for a little while.

After leaving Ashton Lakes, Sven headed his car west on Stickney Point road, crossed over the giant lift-bridge that spanned a magnificent inland waterway, and eventually turned left on prestigious Midnight Pass, the only road leading to the end of the long, narrow key. The drive was enjoyable and the beauty and luxuriousness was not lost on Tanya. It was like a paradise with each estate being more palatial than the one before. Before long, they came to a stop at Sven's favourite haunt. The fast food patio at Turtles Bay was not unlike any other as far as Tanya was concerned. She felt somewhat let down. She didn't know what she expected, but it was more than this.

"I hope ya like it!" offered Sven, as if he had chosen a super-exceptional eatery just for Tanya. Before long, Tanya had forgotten her disappointment. She had also forgotten both diet and protocol as she joined Sven in guzzling large cokes, practically inhaling fries and gravy, and rounding off the meal with double malts.

"This lack of control could cause my self-destruction", laughed Tanya. "Yeah, heart attack on a Styrofoam plate", countered Sven, let's go for the death sentence—a banana split, two spoons!"

"No! Enough is enough, Sven! I haven't done this since I was a teenager!" "Oh! C'mon! We'll swim it off later" he subtly promised.

Like two teenagers, they fought over the maraschino cherry and the last spoonful of ice cream. They talked too loud. They laughed too much, and they definitely ate the wrong kind of food. Back in the car again, Sven purposely drove past the Stickney Point turnoff, heading in the opposite direction from the safety of Ashton Lakes. But Tanya wasn't alarmed. She didn't care. Suddenly she had developed a sense of trust for the handsome man behind the wheel. There was a devil-may-care-ness in the air and she was going along for the ride, maybe looking for quiet miracles. Throwing out a line and hoping to catch happiness.

When the car came to a halt, Tanya found herself facing Siesta Key beach, a sandy stretch on the side of beautiful Tampa Bay. The sight was nothing short of breathtaking and a blanket of wonderland enveloped her as Sven led her along the water's edge. Their feet were caressed by the gentle lapping of the waves as, hand in hand, they strolled along. Before long, Sven casually draped his arm around Tanya's shoulders and, with head thrown back, drank in the salty breeze. It felt so good. So natural. And more than a little comforting. Tanya's world now seemed newly washed. She welcomed the sweet scent of well being. Toronto seemed so far away. Things felt okay. More than just right.

As they walked facing the wind, Tanya inhaled the sea smell, an insidious aphrodisiac for whatever the evening might bring. With each step, Sven's relaxed arm flopped as if disconnected from the rest of his wiry body. The fingers of his left hand plopped softly on Tanya's breast. Whether or not Sven was aware of the strategic location of his fingers and the sensual havoc they were causing, he gave no indication. With heads held high, and smiles on their faces, they silently plodded for miles. The roar of the ocean formed a fitting soundtrack for their wordless trek. Neither spoke. Each was lost in his own paradoxical mixture of sound and silence. But subconsciously, each one of them was negotiating a mutual spot in the other's future.

Eventually, Tanya and Sven turned, and while walking back to the car, they were embraced by one of the most beautiful sunsets on earth. Each wave of Tampa Bay was capped with gold. The salty air they breathed caused an escalated awareness of each other. This awareness, whatever it was, transcended Tanya's problems and caused an exquisite ache to be loved completely. Slipping away was the cloak of chasteness in which she had wrapped herself for so long. This avalanche of emotion was new and overpowering and Tanya was ripe for a new experience. On and on they walked. A man and a woman suspended in time, getting ever closer to the parked car and whatever the night would bring.

Squealing like two delighted children, they raced the last few meters to the car, one trying to outdistance the other. On the way home, Tanya tried to figure herself out. Maybe it had been the combination of the wine and the hot afternoon sun. Drinks can trigger self-defense mechanisms but have also been known to lower our heightened awareness in certain situations. Tanya decided that she fell into the second category.—The 'drink effect' syndrome. So occupied was she, that she didn't realize they were home until the car quietly eased to a standstill in the visitors' parking space.

"Meet ya at ten!" Sven stated matter-of-factly, as Tanya slid out of the car.

"Ten? Where?"

"At the pool of course."

"Nobody swims at ten."

"We're not nobodies!"

Back in her condo, and out from under the magic of Sven and the Siesta sunset, Tanya dispelled any idea of a ten-o-clock liaison. While she had enjoyed the shuffleboard and water badminton in broad daylight with a gang of other people, not to forget the magical walk on the world's purest sandy beach, this was quite another story. And she wasn't ready for dual swimming in the dark with an almost total stranger.

The evening in the condo, patterned on so many others over the last few nights, promised to be long and lonely. And it was so deadly quiet! Tanya wandered aimlessly from empty room to empty room. Every minute seemed an hour long and she was restless. Her thoughts, as usual, fixated on Brad and what he might be doing. She thought of the future they might have had. Confusing thoughts were back. Did she really want to be trapped in the current plight of so many modern females, trying to cope with the marriage-plus-career challenge? Did she want a life circumscribed by 'family first' and focuses which would probably fail to bloom? She really didn't know what she wanted. Her mind chased itself in never-ending circles. She strove to find answers. But could that bring a solution for the romantic misery she now felt? Sometimes, like tonight, Tanya was filled with a bittersweet melancholy. The sweet memory of what she and Brad had shared was offset by the bitterness of never having the chance to see where it might have led.

CHAPTER SIX

Tanya sat as still as a statue, straight and rigid, mulling over options that the night presented. Subconsciously, her eyes sought out the clock every few minutes, and the closer it got to ten p.m., the more ambivalent she became. To swim? Or not to swim? That was the quandary. Almost without thinking, she wandered into the bedroom and slipped into her tiny pink metallic bikini. She had never felt so restless or so lonely. Maybe a walk would do her good. A slow evening stroll would give her time to think. But wait a minute! Who on earth in her right mind would don a bikini in preparation for a late evening walk? God! She must be losing her senses. Nevertheless, she slipped on her beach jacket, wriggled her toes into her thongs, and scooping up the condo keys from the hall table as she went by, quietly let her out into the velvet Florida night.

Tanya hungrily sucked in the humid night air. The night noises and the fragrance of the gardenias intermingled to produce a special magic. She wasn't surprised that her route took her past the clubhouse and into the pool area. Tanya strained her eyes in the darkness trying to detect any movement in or around the pool. Nothing but the humid dark mouth of night. She couldn't seem to stop herself as she continued on, feeling glad that she had decided against the ten o' clock tryst with Sven. It was too clandestine, not her type of thing at all. She was not going to be one of those women, caught up in the game of hide-and-seek, where men inevitably cut to the chase and someone gets hurt along the way. No! She'd had enough hurt and it was still too close to the surface to be anything but painful.

Tanya felt somewhat like a fool as she quietly wandered further into the darkness. But she couldn't seem to stop herself. After rounding the corner of the clubhouse, she placed her jacket carefully over the back of the nearest chair. As she lowered herself, the metal scraped loudly against the cement apron of the pool. She grimaced as she looked around at the darkened condos surrounding the pool. The vaporous night air amplified even the smallest sound. The very end condo had a dimly lit room. Maybe someone couldn't sleep and was passing the hours between the pages of a good book. Maybe someone was looking out from the safety of that condo. The last thing she wanted was to draw attention to herself or her whereabouts. People would think she was crazy, sitting alone at the edge of the pool at ten 0' clock at night. She'd give 'crazy canuck' a whole new meaning.

Traffic noises from Clarke Road were sporadic and muffled, far enough away to create a start-and-stop purring effect. A silver moon sliver provided a special comfort with its minimal illumination, giving an almost surreal glow to the large L-shaped pool. The slight night breeze caused Tanya to shiver. Or was it some kind of anticipation that she couldn't quite come to grips with? She chastised herself for feeling silly. She wanted to move a bit closer to the edge of the pool but couldn't chance scraping the metal chair on the cement again. Speaking of chancing, what if she had taken Sven up on his offer of a night swim? She quietly weighed the option before deciding that it was a situation that might too easily lead into a sexual encounter. She certainly didn't need the complications that sex would bring to the manageable relationship that she and Sven were enjoying

As Tanya sat quietly, her mind sparring came back. Everyone has expectancies from a relationship, she reassured herself. Hers were just different from Brad's, that's all. It would be unnatural if we were all to think alike. Not that it was right or wrong really, but it was a matter of choice and she had made hers. Living with it was the hard part. During her talk with herself, she admitted that she did like the male attention that Sven provided, or to be more exact, his male assurance was doing a great job of counteracting the damage which Brad had caused. Her self esteem had suffered a terrible blow. But, notwithstanding that Sven had affirmed her sexual attraction, was she unwittingly creating an even larger problem?

Sitting stark still in her dark little world, Tanya weighed the pros and cons of the eternal man-woman challenge. The pluses. The minuses. The wins. The losses. And on and on it went. A wheel of 'what goes around comes around'. No solutions. No answers.

A soft plop in the far corner of the pool startled Tanya. Alarm gripped her when she realized that she was not alone. Somewhere in the darkness someone could be watching. An invisible audience was not good. Or safe. Common sense told her to leave. As she stood to leave she was stopped in her tracks by a firm grip on her arm.

"Got your suit?"

Tanya looked up in Sven's face, a face smug with the satisfaction of knowing that he had possessed the power to entice her to the pool.

"I had no intention of swimming!" Tanya answered in a soft stinging voice.

"Oh. I can see that", smirked Sven, looking pointedly at the tiny metallic suit sparkling in the underwater lights of the pool.

"Every woman wears a bathing suit for her evening stroll".

Tanya's look was one of exquisitely cold dislike as she shrugged her shoulders and turned away, indicating an end to the embarrassing discussion. After a short interval of profound awkwardness, Sven tried to calm the waters by launching into small talk. The last thing on earth he wanted was for her to leave. Gradually, he pulled Tanya into the conversation, attempting to carry on as if nothing had happened.

Sven moved to safer grounds via discussion of a workshop that he was to chair on Thursday. An attempt to steer the conversation away from anything personal was necessary if he were to persuade Tanya to stay. Given Tanya's state of mind, Sven went out of his way to limit any chance of controversy. He needed to weigh each word and thought before speaking. Eventually, Tanya eased back into the patio chair, lost in her study of the slender moon sliver cocooned in the velvet darkness of the night.

Tanya had to admit to herself that Sven did, indeed, exude a special kind of appeal and even though she had declined his offer of a quick dip in the pool, her unshakeable terms softened somewhat as he drew a chair up close beside her. Before long, Sven had inched closer. Almost as an afterthought, he nonchalantly draped his arm around her shoulders. Damn those fingers. They were back again. Right at nipple height. Once more they were sending that delicate subtle message. Kick starting latent desire. Driving her crazy as her hormones snapped to attention.

If, for nothing more than getting herself out of the compromising position, Tanya slid out of her beach jacket and strode quickly to the wide concrete steps leading into the tepid water of the pool. But she was not so quick as to be able to hide her erect nipples straining against the metallic threads of her tiny bra. This was not lost on Sven who also made his way into the water. Ever so slowly he waded up behind her, and then encircled her waist with his powerful arms. Tanya could not protest or call out for fear of calling attention of the darkened condos. Helplessly, her silent protest fell prey to Sven's unfair advantage

Gently Sven rocked Tanya to and fro bringing her closer to him each time. Tanya fought the urge to turn and face him. Instead, she battled her heightened hormones as her bottom caressed and re-caressed the growing bulge in Sven's swim suit. It was she who lingered a bit longer on each brief contact, until eventually she found it impossible to control the rhythmic gyration of her hips as she edged her feet apart and lifted her derriere to receive each sexual brush. Before long the rhythmic brushes gave way to calculated thrusts. As of one mind, Sven and Tanya turned in unison to face each other. Quietly they crab-walked to the shallow end of the pool hidden deep in the shadows cast by the majestic palms.

Tanya felt the suggestive flutter of Sven's thumb and forefinger as he gently rolled her nipples. She couldn't believe that he had already removed her tiny bra during the time they had kissed their way to the shadows of the palm. With a feeling of incredible disbelief concerning her own wanton actions, Tanya further shocked herself by cupping Sven's throbbing phallus in one tiny hand while the other hand worked fervently to edge his wet swim suit down over his hips. Working her way to the front of Sven's suit, she struggled to free an endowment that any man would have been proud of. Sven alleviated the problem by raising first one leg, then the other to rid himself of the restraining spandex. Tanya made no effort to suppress her desire as Sven quietly hoisted her up onto the edge of the pool and peeled off her metallic bottoms. His hungry lips found her nipples, worked up to her throat, and finally came to rest on her lips, as he gently lowered her once more into the pool. Sven wedged her legs apart with his knee and crushed up against her. Tanya was overcome by the magic of the night, and the throb of his massive penis, a warm oasis in the coolness of the pool. Each caress was calculated, evoking the emotional response that Sven had anticipated. Sven was an intrepid explorer of women and, to him, Tanya was no exception.

Things had gone too far and it was too late to resort to the tricks that she had perfected and successfully used on Brad. First flirtation, than reservation, and ultimately refusal. But tonight was different and Tanya had no desire to dilute Sven's passion. Maybe this was how things were meant to be. Each kiss was painted with moonlight, underscored by a magic greater than she had ever known. The water lapped softly against their knees as Sven explored and imaginatively carried Tanya to a greater height. The vertical position continued until neither could stem the overpowering sexual pressure. A large thirsty towel received Tanya's wet body as Sven lifted her out of the pool and positioned her, all in one swift movement. Sven mounted swiftly, yet carefully. No whispers of love or halting moments interrupted the frantic initiation. Sven was a well-experienced lover while Tanya filled the role of willing pupil. Each rapacious plunge brought painful pleasure as Sven tested his stamina to the max. Each kiss went on and on as they tasted each other and the sweetness of the night. At long last, they drew apart, pleasantly sated and out of breath. Sven was once again the inherent Romeo, but Tanya was a fully sated woman.

"I didn't think I'd ever feel this way", Tanya simply stated.

"And I didn't think I'd ever feel this way again", came Sven's solemn reply.

Tanya squirmed into her beach jacket, self-consciously stuffing her small bikini into its over-sized pocket. Next she sought out her thongs, declining Sven's invitation to stay and talk awhile. Instead, as she had done the very first time they'd met, she headed for the safety of her condo. She had some serious soul-searching to do. A long serious talk with herself was long overdue.

CHAPTER SEVEN

Passion is a powerful aphrodisiac, an emotion that Brad found himself caught up in as he skied away his days and romanced away his nights. Mitch was, without a doubt, every man's fantasy, an unexpected balm for a devastated heart. And she was his, right here in the flesh, night after thrilling night. Brad delighted in her body and was mesmerized by her fluid movement and the promises emitted from her worldly emerald eyes. Love with its many facets had become a reality as far as Brad was concerned, but Mitch did not share this outlook. To her, love required mega optimism and effort if the plus side were to win. Long ago she had come to the conclusion that the pluses weren't worth the minuses. Until she met Brad, that was.

Intimate dinners, private chats, and the lingering goodnights with Mitch were having a pronounced effect on Brad. Even on the slopes, a place he'd rather be than anywhere else in the world, even during the rigors of the most challenging days, he found himself impatient for the run to be over, bringing him that much closer to the evening and Mitch. Tonight would be special for, at exactly eight pm, prizes and special favours would be presented to those who had performed especially well in the week's activities. Even weekenders and novice skiers were invited to share in the festivities. Because of the award ceremony, rearrangements were necessary and this included moving the evening mealtime to nine o'clock.

Brad rushed through his toilet, eager to be in the ski lodge before Mitch arrived. He chided himself for acting like a schoolboy but he couldn't help it. He took a kind of perverse satisfaction from watching heads turn as Mitch entered the room. Mitch was a woman who had learned to spread her magic and Brad was especially fulfilled, knowing that Mitch was his, a prize he didn't have to share later on. Yup! His life at the moment had become a great big sexual play pen and spurious forces were causing him to misbehave. Brad was walking on air. Mitch was his personal trophy, if only temporarily, and Brad was taking life one evening at a time hoping the bubble wouldn't break.

Time after time he rebuked himself because of his fixation, a situation that seemed to be escalating to a dangerous level. His heart was leading his head and he was deliciously out of control. He had become a willing prisoner of love encased in a body of desire that his mind could not control. He looked forward to each evening and its burgeoning promise of romance.

The ice in Brad's drink was still hard and tinkly by the time Mitch made her appearance. Tonight she looked smashing in powder blue spandex pants topped by a matching turtleneck blouse. Her long hair had been caught up on the top of her head, a wayward tendril or two fashionably caressing either side of her face. A silver shoestring belt clinched her tiny waist. Dangling silver earrings and high-heeled silver shoes with matching evening bag rounded out her ensemble. Brad felt proud, almost chosen, as her eyes searched the room, finally coming to rest on him. She strode directly to his table, using her ample arsenal of female ploys to attract, and then hold the attention of every red-blooded male in the room. She slid into the booth beside Brad, purposely teasing his thigh with her shapely spandex hip. She enjoyed the effect she had on Brad as well as the appreciative glances from his fellow skiers. Every man who looked at Mitch felt lightening-struck, held prisoner by the power of his own physical lust. Emerald eyes and a body to die for were a combination designed to break through even the most resolved male defense. Mitch felt no shame for her power of seduction. Love to her was a noble quest which she believed each of us is entitled to. Long ago she had figured out the exquisite tension of mutual desire that held men and women together. And Mitch considered herself every inch a woman.

Expecting to receive the trophy for top skier again this year, Brad had dressed for the occasion. He proudly wore the sweater of the company sponsoring the team in the prestigious event. He wasn't disappointed when later on, with Mitch proudly watching from the sideline, he did receive, not only Top Skier, but also first prize in both downhill races. These were delicious moments, heady moments that never lost their edge no matter how many awards he received. The excitement combined with the nearness of Mitch allowed Brad's memory to cobweb over, burying even a single thought of Tanya. Thoughts too far removed to emerge, as the long evening played itself out.

Following the wrap up of the awards ceremony, Brad and Mitch hurried to the dinning room. It had been a long day and they were starved. Conversation was sparse as they consumed larger-than-usual portions of roast lamb with mint sauce, baby carrots, and potatoes au gratin. Only a short recess followed before they tackled gateau chocolate, smothered by a generous dollop of the inn's homemade ice cream with chocolate sauce dribbled over the entire dessert for effect. Coffee and their favourite Belgian liquor topped off the delicious meal. The great food, the prizes, and just the special-ness of the day in general had put Brad and Mitch in a celebratory mood. So instead of turning in early, they opted for time together on the soft leather love seat in front of the crackling fire.

"Champagne will help our dinner settle", suggested Brad.
"No doubt about it!" was Mitch's sassy reply.

Crystal glasses clinked as they toasted Brad's skiing achievement and, of course, each other. Several ensuing clinks could be heard as they continued to toast even the silliest of things. As the evening wore on, Mitch removed first her dangling silver earrings and then her silver belt, carefully storing them in her tiny evening bag. Next to go was her silver heels as she burrowed her feet between Brad's thighs for warmth. What an enjoyable way to combat the cold of the drafty old inn. Brad, too, became more comfortable as he let his belt out a notch or two, and again snuggled back into the comfort of the leather sofa. Brad and Mitch sipped champagne. They discussed the obstacles of life. They spoke of pain and disappointment and the gain and loss of love. Before they knew it, they had switched to happier times, times that held no empty spaces. They agreed that love should never be taken for granted, given its fragility and all-too-often transitory status. Their conversation was prolonged and deep. The fire had long since died and the room had emptied save for the two of them by the time Mitch finally slipped into her shoes and led a tipsy Brad through the door and down the familiar drafty hallway.

On the third attempt Mitch managed to get her key into the lock, and Brad not waiting for an invitation this time, followed her inside. After removing his shoes on the mat inside the door, Brad removed the restraining leather belt that had driven him crazy all evening. As he turned to face Mitch, he felt the tentacle of her arm curl around his neck. She pulled him toward her as she stood with her legs firmly planted apart and her back plastered against the wall. Brad was mesmerized by her emerald green eyes and vibrant lips, moist, half open, already in receiving position. Brad cupped Mitch's face in his ands and drew it close to his own. Her tongue teased his lips with swift little darts before boldly sabreing his mouth. Gone was the question of restraint as Brad willingly received the love she offered. Her hand played a ritual of small purposeful circles on his back, gradually making their way ever lower until finally reaching his hips. Ever so gently Mitch rocked him in the cradle of her thighs. Then raising one muscular leg, she encircled his waist, trapping him in her carnal clutch. While she steadied herself on the other leg, her pelvis undulated in slow purposeful circles, gradually increasing in tempo and urgency. Before long, Brad too, took up the sexual rhythm. Brad concentrated on peeling off his heavy sweater while Mitch effortlessly peeled off hers.

Even in the throes of sexual excitement, Brad couldn't help but notice details. He marveled at the tiny erect rosebuds of her breasts as they poked against the creamy lace of her delicate bra. Swiftly he unhooked the bra and bent to hungrily engulf the nearest breast. Mitch seemed to relish the punishment his teeth provided as each undulation drew them across the tender skin of her erect nipples. But Mitch had her own agenda as to how this scene should play out. Relishing the sensation of the heat rising from Brad's fiery groin, she expertly eased his pants and underwear down toward his knees. Taking her lead, Brad tugged at the accommodating spandex of her slacks, quickly baring her undulating hips. Impatiently kicking his pants aside, Brad tried to move toward the narrow bed but Mitch held fast to her position and further secured it by swinging her other leg up to meet the first, forming a circle around Brad's waist. With lace panties still in place, Mitch mashed her vulva against Brad's throbbing groin, her breath becoming ragged as she continued her bombardment of thrusts. Brad forgot about the bed as he impatiently inserted his index finger inside the scanty crotch of her panties. Roughly he pushed the offending satin fabric aside in preparation for the fiery fusion that was sure to come. Brad and Mitch meshed together, each a second skin for the other, plastered together by the moisture of their mounting passion. Finally, unable to restrain himself any longer, Brad positioned his penis directly in the pathway of Mitch's next thrust. Entry was quick and deep as Mitch controlled each plunge bringing mutual satisfaction for them both. Their rut had been quick, climax harmonious. Brad, out of breath and sated, slid with Mitch to the floor, still coupled. Not even the harshness of the mat or the draft of the cold floor could affect the lovers as they lay wrapped in a tight horizontal embrace.

"Thanks. I needed that."

"Me, too! You'll never know how much."

But Mitch was not yet done with Brad and before long she was fondling him again. She toyed with him, patient and expectant, until eventually his erection was firm and ready. Brad felt more than a little pleased with himself and his sexual ability even though it was obvious that Mitch was no stranger to taking the initiative. Brad was happy to fill the role of follower as he allowed himself to be positioned on top of her wiry body. The next phase of their lovemaking was just as satisfactory the first. Face down, balanced on her knees, and rump held high, Mitch invited the long smooth penetration that only this position could assure. Brad, willing but unsure about what was expected of him, permitted himself to be maneuvered into several adventurous positions over the next long hour of multiple orgasms. Mitch seemed insatiable as she finally placed him on his back and rode him to the apex of satisfaction. Drained and happy, Brad collected his things and wobbly made his way to the door. This had indeed been a blue ribbon day, both on and off the slopes.

During the rest of the week a meaningful routine developed between Brad and Mitch. Gruelling challenges were met on the slopes during the day and innovative sexual trysts were carried out during the steamy evening hours. Mitch had undergone a startling metamorphosis since the death of her husband and Brad had gone through his own personal metamorphosis in the span of only a few days. While Mitch provided the sexual fulfillment so sadly lacking in Brad's life since falling in love with Tanya, he had come to fill the role of 'he healthy young man she required to help set her world straight.'

Brad's days were filled with the love of grueling slaloms and his nights were filled with the palpable excitement that only a new experience can bring. He had begun to look at life in a whole new light. He could only remember a few isolated instances in his whole life when he had felt so fulfilled and in control. Sadly, none of them had been with Tanya.

With his hands around ski poles in the daytime and his arms around Mitch at night, Brad was hard pressed to think of any thing more utopian. So besotted he was with Mitch, that he often found himself screaming her name into the wind on his downhill rush to the bottom of the slopes. He was like an adolescent schoolboy, revved by his own hormones and the sexual promise of his every night prom queen. Just the mental image of Mitch was enough to catapult him into a state of burgeoning sexual heat. God, how he wished this utopian situation could go on forever. But he reminded himself that 'forever' could mean a very different thing to different people. Especially to Mitch.

CHAPTER EIGHT

There was no need for her to answer, so he let himself in and prepared to wait while she put the finishing touches on her toilette. At long last, she appeared exuding the residual heat that she never seemed to be without. She looked lovely in black silk lounging pajamas, a vivid contrast to her glowing white skin. Tonight her long hair hung loose, cascading well past her shoulders in large silken waves.

The all-consuming fever that had burned in their initial sexual exploits had gradually given way to a feeling of commitment, one that sex partners come to expect and enjoy. Tonight they had opted for room service and the ambience of the tiny corner fireplace. A small round table had been set up before the fire causing the pre-chilled bottle of wine to bead with sweaty drops. These large tear-like drops created irregular paths down the sides of the bottle before being swallowed up by the thirsty linen napkin. Plump green grapes that popped when bitten into surrounded a perfect circle of soft brie. Soon quail and long grained rice accompanied by a medley of steamed vegetables would follow. Of course, dessert and liquors would serve as the usual prelude to sex. Brad loved food and he loved Mitch. Both were here for the taking.

The illumination of the fire and the dimly lit bedside lamp joined together to embellish the overall setting. Few words were necessary as Brad partially filled each glass and, with raised arm, indicated a silent toast, Mitch followed suit, her eyes brushing Brad's face, before leaning forward and coming to rest, as she locked onto his lips.

"This is happiness!"

"Absolutely!"

With that endorsement out of the way, Brad lathered warm brie on two crackers, one for Mitch, one for himself. Slowly they savoured the or d'oeuvres, before leading into the main course. Wine breaks and toasts punctuated the entire meal. They relished the food and each other. No ghosts had been invited to dine with them this night. Mitch's deceased husband and Brad's lost love were relegated to the distant past as the lovers became completely engrossed with the scene around them and each other.

After the second and final liquor, Brad and Mitch began to quietly disrobe, even taking longer than usual, so as to luxuriate in the electricity that arced between them. There was no urgency. No far-flung clothes. No rush to ravage each other. This was a stark contrast to their initial rutting where clothes had fallen in crumpled heaps as each lover rushed toward his private goal, frantic and shameless in his quest. Both new and not-so-new lovers never lose sight of the fact that sexual satisfaction is a priority for both.

Mitch expertly stroked Brad's body, deliberately downplaying any urgency. This allowed Brad time to put into play all the satisfying techniques she had so patiently taught him. Breathless I-love-you-s punctuated the drawn out foreplay, assuring that when entry came, it would be perfectly timed, deep, and satisfying. Many orgasmic shudders had come and gone before Mitch and Brad lay quietly in the aftermath of their deliberate rendezvous. As Siamese octopi, arms and legs entangled in their net of lust, each provided for the other, a balm for the pain of tortured hearts. By the time Brad roused himself from the warm nest of Mitch's arms, she had already given in to sleep. Brad gazed for a long, long, time at the sleeping woman before him before leaning over her prone form to kiss her goodnight. Again he studied her beautiful face, so relaxed, so content, so completely his. The only sounds in the room were the soft click of the door latch followed by his whispered "! Love you. See you tomorrow."

But tomorrow never came. It was just prior to eight am the next morning when Brad was paged to the lobby to answer an urgent call. What an inopportune time. He had just finished gulping down the last bit of hot coffee before heading out the door to catch the first tow-lift of the day. The call was from his office. They were sorry but they needed him ASAP!

"What do you mean cut my vacation short?"

"There's a computer conference in Florida that just can't wait! They're promoting a brand new concept. Top of the line stuff and we need to get in on the ground floor! We're lucky to have wangled a last minute invitation."

"Can't it wait? At least, till Friday!"

"Fraid not. We need you in the office as soon as you can get here. We've taken the liberty of putting a package together with time, details, flight number, and hotel reservations. You can make up the rest of your holiday time later. Maybe even take an extra few days in the sun for your trouble,"

"Sounds like I have no choice. See ya in a few hours."

"Thanks, guy! We appreciate it. Sorry about the timing!"

Brad reluctantly unbuckled his boots, disappointed about missing a day on the slopes, and more than a bit frantic in his bid to explain to Mitch. He likely would have missed her while taking the phone call and by now she'd be at the top of the mountain, making a face-to-face goodbye impossible. In desperation Brad made one more attempt to call her, but met silence both on the phone and from his raps on her door. Shaking his head in futility, and silently cursing his mother for getting him into the field of computers to start with, he headed to his room to pack.

Randomly throwing his clothes into his two huge suitcases, he tried once more to devise a plan for contacting Mitch. How would she handle this? She didn't have the greatest faith in men as it was! In early afternoon she'd be off the run, anticipating après-ski drinks, a delicious dinner, and of course, an evening of pure romance. She'd be nonplused to say the least. His abrupt departure would be devastating for her. Brad visualized the shock that would register in her clear green eyes. Just when she was beginning to develop a semblance of trust in men, belief would give way to skepticism, then finally to flat-out distrust. She would never believe that he hadn't known in advance when he'd been leaving. Ultimately she'd be angry, madder than hell to have been taken in. She'd scold herself for being such a naïve fool. Even the flowers and the hastily scribbled note wouldn't be enough to do the trick. They would fall on deaf ears. All he could do was to keep trying. Brad felt so helpless, like such a jerk, as he visualized her beautiful face and thought of the unbridled emotions that ruled her life. Most of all, he'd remember her warning—"I told you the night we met that I was no paragon of virtue. I just need a healthy young man to set my world straight!"

Brad stood outside awaiting the shuttle bus that would take him to the airport. Softly falling snow piled onto his shoulders almost as if to bury his sorrow. He sucked a long, long, breath of cold air into his lungs and held it for as long as humanly possible. Subconsciously, he was prolonging his visit to the slopes, tasting a pleasure that had been seriously aborted. He was battling an unquenchable desire as he visualized Mitch, his consolation prize following his breakup with Tanya. All around him happy skiers mushed through the deepening snow of the pathways but he was oblivious. Even the majestic mountains had become blurred and meaningless.

Brad stood stock still. Gone was the caffeine boost that the strong black coffee had provided earlier that morning. It took the second loud blast of the horn from the shuttle bus to startle him out of his reverie. On the bumpy ride to the airport, his precious surroundings dimmed then faded. In their place, Mitch's face appeared, smiling but perplexed. Maybe in her mind their perfect romance had become nothing more than a sexual Armageddon. But Brad was on a shuttle bus and there wasn't a damn thing he could do about it.

CHAPTER NINE

Brad had put in a hellish night after arriving at his office, getting briefed, and rushing through all the necessary details in preparation for his departure to Florida. Several times throughout the evening he had made frantic calls to Mitch but all remained unanswered. It well past midnight by the time Brad fell into bed, frustrated, disappointed, and incredulously helpless when it came to Mitch. Second guessing revved up. Maybe he should have refused to cut his holiday short. How could the Company expect him to just jump and run at a moment's notice? One thing that he knew for sure was that he didn't want to be the man that disappointed Mitch, stripping her of the last anchor that life held out to her.

Early the next morning, after a harrowing night, Brad was on the 'red eye' flight feeling leaden, going through the motions so to speak. The night before had been hellish to put it mildly. He must have awakened at least twenty times. Every time, he had thought of Mitch, and he reminded himself that she was not the kind of woman who would allow anyone to tamper with her ego. He also knew that he didn't have a hope in hell of getting her to understand. Clearing customs smoothly, and with time left over, he once again raced to the nearest phone, desperate to contact Mitch. His heart lurched expectantly with each long ring, but ultimately he hung up, dejected and disappointed.

Two and a half hours latter, Brad entered the lavish conference room of the Florida Holiday Inn. He seated himself near the back and took the opportunity to peruse the materials his office had so hastily thrown together. As he read the brochure, he could see why his boss had been so excited. The speaker who would present the latest concepts re Computers and the Future was a forty-two year old heavy hitter well established in the department of sales. His successful workshops had put him away out front. He was widely known and there wouldn't be one potential buyer who could ignore his expertise.

Sven was a rising star in the Ultex Company and his sure-fire performances had become legionary. His success preceded him as the 'somebody' who the company turned to when a spectacular sales pitch was needed. Brad was anxious to see just what his bag of goodies held. He was deep into his material preparation when a tap on his shoulder caused him to look up into the face of, whom else, but the keynote speaker. With exaggerated courtesy, he welcomed Brad to Florida, the presentation, and last but not least, a private cocktail party following the presentation. "Don't forget now, Rm. 406." Brad thanked him, secretly grateful for being rescued from the long lonely evening that, no doubt, stretched ahead. Only last night, before leaving Toronto, Brad had practically begged Tanya's sister, Alicia, to give him Tanya's Florida phone number. But 'no go'. She hung tough to her promise to Tanya. Angry and disappointed, Brad was gripped by a wave of powerlessness. These feelings had intensified upon landing at the Sarasota aeroport. He had felt a profound sense of frustration but there hadn't been a damn thing he could do about it. Here both he and Tanya were, in the same general area, but they might just as well have been continents apart.

Brad's mind twisted and turned and went around in circles. Pride, by now, was irrelevant and it paled beside his need to reestablish with Tanya if for no other reason than to apologize and to make up for his childish cruelty. Although he had come to Sarasota to take advantage of the computer presentation, the whole arrangement was fast becoming overshadowed by the resurrection of Tanya thoughts. The feelings of pain and suffering, that Mitch had taken such care to help him bury, albeit temporary, were back.

As the seats filled up, Sven took unusual care to welcome the participants, treating each as if he were by far the most important. Client after client was given the special treatment as Sven, adapt at saying the right thing at the right time, made sure his pizzazz was not wasted on this hand-picked group of potential buyers. His ability to think on his feet had been with him since childhood and now, as an adult, he effortlessly dealt with the minutiae of advanced computer technology, and of course, the terms of payment. There was no need to feel the fear of failure. He had a profound sense of self confidence and knew his message would not fall short. He had passed those tests a long time ago.

Once the meeting was called to order, Sven quickly established dominance over the entire room. He trotted out his warm friendly smiles, interspersing them throughout his familiar well-rehearsed spiel. Using his voice and his body language to an ungodly degree, he worked the room. Self-assured and positive of upcoming sales, he smiled himself toward success. Even the diehards fell prey to his persuasiveness and escalating volume. Sven dragged each and every non-believer into his computer net, compelling them to believe, accept, and above all buy! Dialogue was tailor-made, pared to convince each client, as he shepherded his audience through the morass of product guarantee. Of course, he ended on a high note, hands outstretched and held high, and his smile infectious and compelling. Lastly came the inevitable handshakes as another successful workshop drew to a close.

Because Sven was not one to leave anything to chance, the cocktail party was twofold in that it was an obligatory part of the presentation as well as the official end of his Florida business-cum-pleasure stay. Potential buyers swarmed around Sven, bombarding him with questions concerning estimations and return projection. When time for thinking was required, he deliberately slowed the tempo by handling each customer's concern in a slow thought-provoking manner. His demeanor was always genuine and unwavering right up to the very end. Sven was unflappable as he catered to exactly the sort of people who were prepared to take a chance. They counted on Sven to help them decide which computer materials would be vital in an ever-growing competitive world market.

Sven's sales pitches were by no means something he took for granted and were more often than not apt outlets for his adrenalin highs. He never forgot his earlier days when sales had not always been forthcoming, days that he had come to consider hollow. Hungry days that he must always remember! But those days were long since gone and it had been ages since he'd felt the need to beat himself up.

CHAPTER TEN

Tanya, accompanied by Bob and Vonne, arrived well in advance of the cocktail party and, at Vonne's insistence, quietly slipped into the back of the conference room. Tanya was anxious to catch Sven in action. She certainly wasn't disappointed as she stared in rapt attention as Sven swiveled, first to one side of the room, then the other, drawing heavily upon his charisma as he appealed to the buyer instinct in each potential customer. A rush of sexual fantasy overtook her as she watched her private master of manipulation. She felt so proud just to be part of the intimate group before him.

Sven seemed born to perpetual motion, fired by the special kinetic energy so necessary in all high-level sales performances. Tanya, as well as the audience, was connected to the message he so aptly sent. Sven, never one to miss a trick, had been surprised to see the arrival of Tanya and her party. He thought she looked especially beautiful and ached to rush over and welcome her. He wanted to thank her for showing such interest in his seminar.

Down deep, he had to admit to himself that he was glad of the opportunity to show off his stuff. But it was hardly an opportune time to approach her, especially when flanked by dozens of keenly interested clients. Despite the flattery that Tanya felt by being connected to a male of Sven's importance, an unwelcome sense of uneasiness was creeping in. This pronounced discomfort caused her to re-think the cocktail party which lay ahead. After weighing the pros and cons, Tanya leaned over to Vonne and whispered her change of mind. Vonne, the world's greatest party girl, would have none of it and drew attention by making a not-so-subtle fuss.

Unbeknown to Tanya, Sven wasn't the only man in the room with a special interest in her, for it was at that moment that Brad glanced in the direction of the commotion. He studied the noisy trio, especially the girl who closely resembled Tanya. But this girl, as opposed to Tanya, had a well developed sense of who she was and what she wanted. Shock registered when she turned to persue her conversation with her friends, for indeed it WAS Tanya. At a computer workshop yet! Brad sat still, trying very hard to convince himself that Tanya's presence was of no concern to him. But it wasn't working. He became flushed, almost panicky. He was very uncomfortably aware, not only of Tanya, but also of Sven. The effect of his magnetism was obvious as Brad watched him approach Tanya and casually pull her aside.

Brad commiserated, feeling the outrage of helplessness, as he agonized about how to approach the woman he loved. He continued to agonize as his hot flash of intention fizzled, then died, much like their relationship that had burst at the seams on the morning he sent the irretrievable fax. Maybe he should just rush up and blurt out a spontaneous apology before he lost his nerve. Let the chips fall where they may. But basic prudence took over as he watched how Tanya proudly basked in the warmth radiated by Sven. It required super-human effort for Brad to get his unbridled emotions in check.

Brad bided his time waiting for Sven to move on. He was desperate to approach Tanya. Brad thought of how he had come to terms with the loss of sex and the special-ness of the remedial intimacy that he and Mitch had shared. Her zest for living had infected him, inoculating him against failure, be it on the slopes, in the office, or on the narrow cot they had so hungrily shared in the drafty ski chalet. He re-lived the frustration he felt in his failure to reach Mitch, to explain, to apologize, and to assure her that what they had was meaningful. But he had to admit that their time spent together was becoming illusionary as, day after day, his repeated attempts to reach her failed.

At long last Sven moved from Tanya's side, beckoned by two or three zealous clients. A familiar flutter of uncertainty prodded Brad into action and he found himself walking towards the most attractive woman in the room. Tanya looked up as she felt the familiar hand cup her elbow. As she looked into Brad's eyes, her smile turned to plastic, becoming nothing more than one of those replacement smiles we all carry around with us in case of emergency.

"Tanya, I'm surprised to see you here—pleasantly surprised, that is!"

Her smile now faded completely, pushed aside by an incredulous look of disbelief. Memories of their special bond of the past flooded over her, but then, so did the memory of the painful fax. Quickly, she recovered her composure and became the epitome of indifference.

"I didn't know you had such an interest in computers. Quite a lively group don't you think?" Brad continued.

Tanya's look was one of cold rejection, the fax message still solidly embedded in her mind. The emotional strain was palpable as the one-time lovers fought to regain their dignity. Brad could see that Tanya was not the girl he had left behind. The woman before him had a well developed sense of where she was headed. She exuded the confidence that only newfound individuality could provide. Surprising as it might seem to Brad, she resisted him quite readily. He tried hard to play down the effect that Tanya's rejection had on him, but despite his Herculean effort to keep his emotions in check, he was nervous and off balance. Sven, business-like to a fault, still worked the room, spreading his magic, but out the corner of his eye he didn't fail to notice Tanya talking to the tall Canadian stallion whom he had greeted prior to the presentation. She appeared anxious as she moved away from the handsome stranger who seemed to have more than a passing interest in her.

CHAPTER ELEVEN

As the clients rallied around Sven, greeting him with vigorous bonhomie, Brad seized the chance to engage Tanya in further conversation. He quietly closed the distance between them.

"Please, Tanya, we must talk"

"Why? Is your fax machine broken?" she asked sarcastically.

"Tanya, just a few minutes, Okay?"

His words were lost as Tanya deftly moved away. Just as life was beginning to get bearable, here was Brad digging up bones. And she wanted none of it! She considered his approach nothing less than a moderate level of seduction. She fought to control herself, using every ounce of effort she could muster. She had to think and act in a rational manner. It was no time to let her emotions get away on her. Brad's presence had put a new spin on things and Tanya knew there was only one remedy to the uncomfortable situation in which she found herself.

Tanya was almost to the door when Sven stopped her. She looked up into his face, the face of a brilliant lecturer to the people all around her. But to her, he was just a man with strong feelings, a man teetering on the shaky path that inevitably leads to love.

"I need you. The cocktail party needs you", Sven whispered, trying to sound casual. To the rest of the room he announced, "Cocktails in 406. More pleasure than business!" Tanya felt flattered but uneasy. What if Brad had also been invited? How could she handle both Brad and Sven in the same room at the same time? She had noticed earlier that Brad, too, had shared her ill-at-ease-ness. Even manipulating the hands on computer materials, an everyday occurrence for him, had proven laborious. Little did Tanya realize that the excitement of seeing her once again had dissolved every shred of bravado that Brad had so valiantly tried to portray?

A sharp twinge of sympathy gripped Tanya as she sensed Brad's discomfort. She stole a secret sideways glance at his pain but her view was blocked by Sven as he persistently squeezed between them. He pulled her to him and whispered, "Please indulge me. You won't be sorry. I promise." The special electricity that Sven had ignited at the pool just a week or two ago was back and Tanya felt mortified to feel her face redden. She felt a social dislocation taking hold as her passive resistance slowly drained away. Once again she composed herself and adapted to the occasion at hand. Her manicured fingertips reached toward Sven's outstretched hand in a show of dubious acceptance.

Tanya was glad she had taken such extra-special care with her appearance. Her hair was perfect. Her pale pink cotton dress fitted her like a glove. Tiny pearl earrings and a matching pearl brooch, pinned to her left lapel, complimented the pastel pink. She had tried on outfit after outfit before deciding that looking understated was preferable to the brightly coloured cottons which the Floridians thought so chic. The real reason for her wardrobe choice had nothing to do with style really. As usual, because she was basically shy, she had learned to downplay anything that drew attention to her. But that was the other Tanya. Now she had decided to change all that. No more melting into the crowd. She would now be someone to be reckoned with. And there wasn't a man in the room who wouldn't agree. Her blonde hair was almost white which provided a nice contrast for her tawny brown skin, both compliments of the Florida sunshine. The combination was breath-taking, one that caused men to sit up and take notice. Nor was it lost on Sven who proudly squired her into the cocktail party that was already in progress.

CHAPTER TWELVE

The party was small but lively, sprinkled with everybodies, each talking louder than the next, each promoting his personal opinion that demanded an immediate audience, or feedback at the very least. Sven soon found himself in the unenviable position of trying to strike a balance between fulfilling his role of host and at the same time arranging undivided time for Tanya. Several times he covered the distance between himself and Tanya, ever ready to seek out the advantage of a quiet corner. During these brief interludes, he teased her shoulders with his lips, and meaningfully squeezed her hand. He stared deep into her eyes, his own holding the promise of 'later on'.

Tanya was confused, not sure, and what Sven planned as a quick romantic interlude interpreted into an awkward silence. Tanya didn't know if she was ready for a re-enactment of their earlier poolside tryst. Images of Brad kept getting in the way, causing her to brood and fidget. Her female intuition warned her to take her time. Go slow. Only lately had she been able to form opinions. But Sven's influence on her was blatant. And he was not a man who allowed him self to be tortured by love. He dealt on an adult level leaving no time for a little-girl woman who should have learned a long time ago to cope with the everyday compromises so rift in the adult world. Tanya knew she could never resort to the tricks she had pulled on Brad. First her flirtatious smile, then reservation, and finally refusal. She cringed as she thought of the times she had dampened the flame of Brad's advances, diluting his passion time and time again.

Intuitively, Tanya knew that while Brad was still willing to be a maintenance man for her long-term happiness, Sven lived for the moment. Self-satisfaction was the name of his game. Trying to escape the dilemma in which she found herself, Tanya readily accepted one cocktail after another from the waiter's passing tray. She was determined to obliterate the feeling of near panic, a feeling that had been escalating since Brad's arrival. She was well aware of Brad's lengthy conversation with the attractive buyer from Seattle. Both Brad and the Seattle buyer were here specifically at Sven's request. She watched as the attractive girl touched Brad's arm to make a point. Tanya reminded herself that she shouldn't care. She was through with Brad. But her eyes kept straying back time and time again. Was the girl's hand lingering longer each time she touched Brad? Or was her imagination playing tricks on her? It's so unfair, she thought, even when the affair was over, it really wasn't over. And here she was paying for it with a painful moral hangover.

Introductions, handshakes, and backslaps befitting the occasion, kept pace with the escalating consumption of alcohol. Acquaintances became best friends, suggestion became fact, and promise to keep in touch became paramount as the buyers melded into a tight homogenous group. This group was held together by the glue of computer interest and was buoyed up by the electric ambience of the party. Tanya knew very well that she was drinking too much but she needed the alcohol to tranquilize her scampering thoughts. She stood alone, battling her emotions, taking advantage of the time to reflect. Sven was once again drawn into a mini-discussion about software, delivery, and fiscal year returns. Brad and the attractive Seattle buyer had moved even closer, locked in the world of deep computer conspiracy. Tanya suddenly felt left out and unimportant, just as she had so many times in the ski chalets. Maybe it was her. Maybe there was something she was not doing right. Her eyes moved to Sven, studying his perfect frame and remembering the private fiery intimacy they had so recently shared. She wrestled with her feelings of uncertainty. Given the chance, she wondered whether or not she wanted Sven to remain in the perfect 'one time 'love category or to become a permanent thread in her petit point of life.

And Brad? What about him? Had he merely become a habit? A normal first-love fixation? Now just a memory? On the other hand, she could not dispel the chemistry she still felt when earlier in the evening he had approached her in an effort to pursue a conversation. Lovers, even past lovers, have a tendency to forgive or downplay the bad times. They do this in order to elevate the good times and Tanya understood this. She understood that she and Brad would have to face many disturbing, even gut-wrenching facts, if reconciliation was ever to come about. Could they pick up and go on? And marriage? Wasn't trust the primary basis for anything as serious as wedded bliss? Attitude was a big one too. She knew she had changed. Gone was the puritan attitude that she had embraced for so long. Sven and a velvet Florida night had taken care of that. Gone, too, were the little-girl woman and her inept attempts to make adult decisions. Instead here stood a wiser, albeit still uncertain, woman. Tanya always had, and still did, place Brad in the trustworthy category. But as the image of Sven sliced through her mind, she wondered if she could ever really trust herself.

The party continued to bubble all around her as Tanya re-lived the devastation of her love affair with Brad. She weighed the pros and cons of everything and everybody. Would she and Brad ever be able to salvage anything? Could they blow life into the ashes of their love? Maybe even rekindle the few weak embers that remained. Maybe even make it work this time. The comparisons set in again. Sven was driven by his burning desire to push ahead, be top dog in his chosen field. Brad, on the other hand, thanks to his mother, was stuck in a field not of his choosing. This, however, enabled him to save his biggest efforts for the challenge of the slopes. But both men shared similarities and differences. They were exceptionally handsome despite the considerable age difference. Given their widely different perspectives, they were hard to compare in some categories. Sven treated adultery as adult pastime, while Brad had always considered it improper unless sheathed in the confines of marriage or, at the very least, a committed personal relationship.

As Tanya accepted another drink, she felt torn between a possible reconciliation with Brad or a replay of her passionate nights with Sven. She knew she had to choose one or the other, because together she would be facing an emotionally dangerous situation. Drawn to the verbal bantering on her right, wild flashes of sexuality, pure in form, lightning-ed across her mind as she watched Sven throw back his head and laugh obligingly at a joke told to the group by a big time buyer. Her loins grew hot as she mentally envisioned what lay beneath his silk shirt and the finely-textured slacks he wore. Brad's willingness to pursue her, to wait until she readied herself for sex if necessary, only magnified her immediate problems. Tanya was fairly certain that Brad had only dated one girlfriend before dating her so who knows what his sexual performance might be. She had denied him the opportunity of experiencing lovemaking to the fullest although their petting sessions had been steamy and hot.

Tanya wasn't the only one at the cocktail party who was ill at ease. Brad, too, tossed back another drink and was careful to keep as far away from Tanya as possible. Flashes of Mitch, an uncomplicated woman, lit up his mind. He allowed himself a temporary lapse into his world of emotional fragility. The bottom line was that he was still drawn to Tanya like a magnet. He silently devoured her immaculate body, a body which showed no outward signs of the recent stress that the trauma of the fax surely must have caused. Her presence stood out in the crowd as she eventually moved within the circle of her rowdy friends. She seemed cool and collected, unaffected by the din all around her. Buyers continued to crowd around Sven who encouraged their questions while, at the same time, allowing his eyes to seek out and lock with Tanya's. His eyes spelled out a strong sensual message, a promise of what the evening could and surely would bring.

The closer Brad edged toward Tanya, the more he felt his bravado fail. Shifting sands of uncertainty overwhelmed him as he feared her cold rejection. He worried about his ability to stand up under the cross examination that would surely come. Despite his uncertainty, Brad felt compelled to at least take a stab at resurrecting their old passion. It was almost as if an invisible hand was pulling him along. Tanya could feel Brad's presence as he inched ever closer. He was akin to a dietary supplement for someone like herself who was convalescing from the ravages of love gone wrong. The only barrier between Brad and Tanya was distance which was slowly being minimized. People were watching which made her feel vulnerable, too vulnerable to be anything but cordial. But Sven's eyes were on patrol again and it was sabotaging her comfort level to an unbearable degree. Tanya attempted to settle her dilemma by moving quietly to a small table in the corner. She sat down and carelessly crossed her legs, more concerned with her predicament than her hemline. The exposure of her shapely thighs was not wasted on either Brad or Sven. While Brad was thinking for the hundredth time about his approach strategy and their chance of a possible future together, Sven was riveted to the sight of Tanya's voluptuous body, already planning the amorous night that lay ahead.

Brad rose slowly to his feet. His head ached from the excessive drinks. He was a man filled with pain, both physical and emotional. He was too full of unsaid words and unshed tears, but more importantly, he was filled with misgivings, a victim of his own rash behaviour. He should never have sent the fax and now the time had come to set things straight. He moved toward Tanya, not stopping until he was directly in front of her. She glanced up and was suddenly held by the hurt reflected from a face frozen with sadness. "I'm sorry about the fax, Tanya, and I truly hope you can forgive me", he blurted out. Tanya could not trust herself to speak, so merely nodded before turning away. Her anger was beginning to melt away. Maybe the stupid fax was not such a big deal after all. But she needed time to think. Time to be alone.

Brad paused uncertainly then headed for the door. He felt better and worse all rolled into one. Tanya watched him walk away. Now it was her turn to feel like a prisoner held ransom by the hurt she had obviously caused. Brad's pain had shaken her, leaving her oddly depressed. She took no satisfaction from hurting Brad but the fax fiasco was etched firmly in her mind. The cruelty of the hasty act had made her look and feel like a fool. It had also served to undermine Brad's integrity. He was not the type of person who should have behaved in such a manner. Even so, when Brad left, she felt a huge emptiness. She longed for their special love that had gone so terribly wrong.

CHAPTER THIRTEEN

Tanya nestled back into the soft leather of the passenger seat as Sven closed her door before taking himself around to the driver's side. The roof of the sleek white convertible was down, increasing her awareness of the familiar Floridian sounds and smells. The night jumped into focus as Tanya's mind continued to reel from the trauma of meeting and actually speaking to Brad. Worse still, the presence of both Brad and Sven at the cocktail party caused a terrible pressure, in turn causing Tanya to pressure herself. She had battled the indecision of whether to at least give Brad the benefit of a conversation or quietly leave without him. Or should she leave with Brad? Or do the proper thing and go home with Sven? Her questions had been answered when Brad had headed for the door. Shivering from the impact of it all, Tanya pulled her cardigan tightly around her shoulders, laid her head back on the cool headrest, and closed her eyes.

As the car slid swiftly through the night, Tanya wrestled with the demons of indecision. She had been civil to Brad, painfully so, when he had approached her earlier in the evening. The image of a broken heart filled her mind. Maybe she had over reacted. She was still stung by the hurt of the fax, a circumstance which considerably strengthened her resolve not to be fooled a second time. But here she was riding home with Sven, her mind in turmoil as anger and desire mingled with self-recrimination. Thoughts were tumbling through her mind like leaves in a hurricane as Sven brought the car to a quiet stop in the condo guest parking lot.

The hour was late and the complex almost totally asleep. The fragrant peace was disturbed only by the white cat and the sound of their footsteps as they made their way to the darkened condo. Sleep would be a long time coming tonight, Tanya thought, as she slipped her key into the door. Once inside, Sven slid his arms around Tanya's neck, fingers familiarly resting just above her nipples, enjoying the smooth curves of her well-defined body. Tanya moved slightly ahead as she pushed the door closed. Once inside, she attempted to shrug off the pleasure Sven's fingers brought, as well as his control over her emotions. She needed time to dissect the worrisome developments of the last few hours. But Sven was once again up close, playfully pulling her toward him. She found herself subconsciously responding as he cuddled her from behind in a gentle sexual wrap. Involuntarily, Tanya molded her uplifted bottom to Sven's throbbing groin. Suddenly, she caught herself. This was a repeat performance of what had led to their sexual encounter to begin with and she was far too confused at this point in time to continue down the inevitable road to sex.

Tanya's emotions ran the gauntlet from Brad's sad eyes to Sven's familiar fingers. Eyes! Fingers! Men! Body parts! Emotions! Brad or Sven? That was the kaleidoscopic decision. Tanya agonized over the disturbing choice before concluding that a decision was impossible. Sven, sensing her ambivalence, slowly drew away and made his way to the built-in bar. Casually selecting matching frosted glasses, he laid the foundation for a romantic nightcap. Sven did not appreciate being rebuffed. It was not his style at all. His life, for the last five years anyway, had become fast-paced and interwoven by chance encounters with interesting women. His relationship with Tanya was par for the course, something to pass the time and make the Florida experience memorable for the both of them.

Sven was surprised, perhaps concerned, that despite being denied sex during their last two encounters, Tanya had a serious hold on his day-to-day thoughts. Usually his common sense took over and he moved on to greener pastures. He was more than a little annoyed with himself as he found his ability to get what he wanted taking second place to his desire to please Tanya and pursue their relationship. Sven chose an easy chair closest to the bar and elevated the footrest to a comfortable level. By now Tanya had slid into the chair facing him. Holding the tiny crystal glasses high, they toasted each other with delicious Belgian liquor.

"Cheers!"

"Ditto!"

Sven had no intention of allowing Brad to jimmy him into second spot. He had faith in himself. Wasn't his workshop proof of his ability? Yes, he was an ultimate player, a man with a penchant for doing things his way. Sven was comfortable in his own skin and, even if he could, he wouldn't change a thing.

Tanya quietly sipped the sweet milky chocolate as she again considered her dilemma. It was true that Sven had awakened her as a woman while Brad had been content to wait. She preferred Sven's aggressive style to Brad's passivity. Or did she? Already she regretted her refusal to talk things out with Brad and she was haunted by the sadness and rejection mirrored in his eyes as he left the party. But, on the other hand, she couldn't deny that Sven's arrogance held a certain fascination for her. Each sip of liquor heightened her confusion. She couldn't help but admire Sven's zest for living. It was a trait that never failed to inject a specialness into their nightly encounters. Sven leaned forward, close enough to stroke Tanya's bare arm with his index finger, perfectly aware of the pleasurable tingle he was creating. Tanya adjusted her position ever so slightly as she neither wished to encourage nor offend him. But Sven's motive was abundantly clear. There was no doubt that they both knew where this was designed to take them. As Sven's strokes became even more sensual, her heartbeat quickened and the temperature of the room became unbearably warm. Again persistent comparisons leapt into Tanya's mind. Sven, vital self-assured Sven, expected to get exactly what he wanted. Unlike Sven, Brad loved her unconditionally. Surely that counted for something. Didn't it?

By midnight Tanya's conflict has not lessened. She still hadn't come to terms with her feelings of Sven versus Brad. To make matters worse, Sven's persistence was showing signs of impatience. Tanya felt annoyed by his presumptuous attitude, but at the same time, felt double-crossed by her own anticipatory urges. By now Sven's index finger had become a whole hand. A hand with a mission, that was. Sven now stroked the entire length of her arm, making sure the back of his hand caressed the side of her breast in passing. The old sense of excitement was back, catapulting itself to a dangerous level. Tanya did not, could not, remove his hand. She see-sawed between the ecstasy that Sven held out and the palpable sadness she had seen in Brad's eyes earlier that evening. She wished to god she'd never come to Florida. In fact, she wished she'd never taken a vacation at all. Things had been so much simpler, never mind happier, when everybody understood the game plan. This was her first foray into the emotional arena where subtle rules were subject to shift and change. Here, circumstances altered cases. Maybe it was the country. Maybe it was the man. Maybe it was the liquor. Or was it just the magic of the night? Whatever it was, Tanya wasn't ready for it. She wasn't up to the demands of Sven's sexual expectancies, or the nagging regret she had brought upon herself concerning Brad. Tanya stood up and took Sven's hand, tugging him gently to his feet. After a brief moment of embarrassment, she whispered goodnight.

"Surely you must be kidding", replied Sven, speaking for himself and his unsatisfied male assemblage.

"Fraid, not. I'm tired and it's very late. Tomorrow is another day!"

Emptiness of the evening ahead haunted Sven as he contemplated the unexpected move. Everything had gone so smoothly until now. His workshop had been nothing short of successful. The follow-up cocktail party had been the piece-de-resistance, rounding out a perfect business venture. The end of this perfect day for Sven should have provided a mutual feeling of sexual satisfaction. But you win some, you lose some, he reminded himself. And tonight he hadn't won.

Sven was determined to hide the cost of the emotional burden Tanya had caused by reminding himself that he could always call upon his laser focus to find a replacement for her. The world was full of gullible women who were no match for such a titan of testosterone as himself. Sven loved himself, not only as a competitive businessman, but also as a test-proven predator of love. It was, by now, second nature to him to flaunt his body and his resources, causing girls to gravitate toward him. And they stayed for as long as it took his libido to pave the way to pure romance. Tanya's rejection tonight was nothing more than a temporary snag. It was hurtful but not fatal. Her love or lack of it did not equate to a terminal blow. He'd just turn in early, get a good night's sleep and see what tomorrow would bring.

At home in bed alone, Sven considered his options. He could always seek another non-threatening female to fill the void and/

or rebuild the walls of his comfort zone. He needed meticulous walls that sheltered his real motives. His personal-planning strategy included handshakes that put small bones at risk as well as touches as gentle as a whisper. No matter which, he knew he was not one to be ignored. His body language translated into power and he used it as an aphrodisiac. Yet tonight he'd been brought to his knees by a beautiful naïve Canadian. Maybe he was losing his touch. Getting too complacent. Maybe he'd spent so much time cultivating his own personal assets that he'd forgotten to harvest hers. Oh well, he had no intention of belaboring this rare rebuff. Gradually he fell into a fitful sleep. But even in sleep he wore his infectious grin, undoubtedly planning the most affective way to approach his next 'client'.

CHAPTER FOURTEEN

Tanya readied for bed, opened her window to take advantage of the balmy night air, before comfortably settling back into the large soft bed. She idly thought of the old western song, Sleeping Double in a Single Bed, and thought how it applied to her. Sleep did not come. She tossed and turned and listened to the muted sounds from the night outside. Florida nights were so warm, so moist, and so romantic. Tanya tried to distract herself with everything from planning tomorrow to deep-breathing exercises in hope of heralding sleep, but it was all to no avail. A slow burn, just a tingle at first, was now escalating to a pronounced feeling situated deep in her groin area. Maybe she had been too hasty in dismissing Sven. She needed someone to hold and comfort her. Drive the loneliness back. Make things okay. She wondered if it was too late to change her mind as far as Sven was concerned. Maybe he wasn't sleeping either. Could or should she call and just invite herself over? Quickly, she dispensed with the idea, chastising herself for being so blatantly wanton.

Tanya stared at the ceiling fan as it twirled in the lazy night air. She thought of Brad. He had been the love of her life but not necessarily the man of her dreams. She was confused. She needed an omega3 man to shore up her anemic love life. Or did she? Just a short time ago, Brad had been her whole life. True, there hadn't been an over abundance of passion and fire but that had been the result of her own old-fashioned ideals. But she was a different person now. She knew the difference and there was no turning back. While Brad felt comfortable in his own skin, she had wanted to spread her wings and fly.

Twenty minutes had passed before Tanya decided that her personal fire had to be extinguished. For her, this was a novel feeling and she wasn't quite sure how to handle the situation. But her emotions had a mind of their own and she soon found herself slipping into her short terry robe. Her feet found their way into matching thongs as she quietly headed down the hall. With house key in pocket and a fire to be quenched, she let herself out into the romantic Florida night. She made her way down the pathway, crossed the visitor parking area, and finally picked her way through the fragrant azalea bushes flanking the entrance to Sven's darkened unit.

Sven answered her first timid tap on his screen patio door for, he too, had awakened, thirsty and restless, and was sitting quietly in his lanai sipping cool fresh grapefruit juice. Tanya felt foolish as he wordlessly guided her through the dimly lit hall to the lanai. He gently pulled her down on his lap. She trembled as bare bottom was assaulted by the initial stirrings of his enormous erection. Sven nonchalantly untied the belt of her terry robe and slide it off her shoulders. In one smooth motion, his mouth engulfed her nearest nipple. Only the sounds of his hungry sucking mouth disturbed the fragrant night around them. Before long, both partners moved in rhythm as Sven's phallus, now fully erect, prodded the moist triangle of Tanya's body, demanding to be let in.

Without disengaging his lips, Sven quickly swung Tanya around to straddle him. Gently he placed both hands under her buttocks, spreading her legs far apart as he lowered her onto his massive penis. Although she could hardly accommodate the length or girth of his manhood, she could not stop herself from bearing down, corresponding to the ever-increasing thrusts. She felt a delicious pain, a kind she had never felt before but did not want to end. Sven continued to forcefully plunge her body up and down all the way. His tongue, in perfect harmony, plunged deep into her gasping mouth as he drove himself deep inside. Her womanhood, taut but receptive, fielded every thrust as they brutally rode each other to a consummate climax

For a long time, neither Sven nor Tanya moved. The only interaction was the sharing of the grapefruit juice as they passed the glass back and forth, trying to quench their insatiable thirst. Despite the fact that Tanya felt that something still filled her, a persistent residue of fire still remained. Before long, Tanya and Sven were once again entwined. There was no need to break the silence with mere words as they dueled sexually, each combatant striving to attain exquisite satisfaction. Soon breaths quickened and positions changed with kaleidadescopic speed as they copulated again and again. The final frame of their rut was almost masochistic as Tanya broke all barriers between herself and sexual satisfaction. She had forevermore closed the doors to girlish innocence.

The sky was a pinkish-blue as Tanya woke and prepared to leave. Her subtle movements had awakened Sven who slowly rolled over and pulled her back under the tangled sheets. Although Tanya felt somewhat worse for the wear as a result of the last night's sexual acrobats, she nevertheless complied, happy just to cuddle and nestle into the haven of Sven's arms. But Sven had other plans. The man was beyond belief and his erect manhood was proof of it. Before long his excitement rubbed off on Tanya as she found herself preparing for another sexual assault. She welcomed him, gradually taking the lead, as they devoured each other shamelessly. No orifice was left untouched as they consumed each other for what would be their last time.

CHAPTER FIFTEEN

Brad was lonely and disappointed, and being banished to the doldrums of the office was certainly no help. He found the days long and troublesome, plagued by his inability to obliterate the memory of Tanya. Since encountering her in Florida, her presence had especially haunted him. In fact, he was consumed by the nagging ache left by far too many unanswered questions. For the life of him, he couldn't understand her refusal to at least talk things out. It was to her benefit, as well as his, to address the personal stake each had in the other's future. Why not let yesterday just be a cancelled cheque and start over unencumbered by past differences? He saw no need to shred the past and much preferred to emphasize the special love they had once shared. In between his 'Tanya' thoughts, snapshots of Mitch assailed him. He loved the way that Mitch lived, filling each day with Teutonic efficiency so as not to waste a moment. She was alive and well and living to dance another day. She lived by the code of velvet nights and superlative relationships. Mitch had written a manual on how to handle failed relationships. She had taken a sabbatical from marriage and now sailed through life allergic to conflict.

Before long, Brad's thoughts were back on the Tanya trail. He couldn't stop thinking about the obvious change he'd noticed in her. It concerned him. No, it bothered him really. Unlike Mitch who harbored an abiding distrust of men, the Tanya he remembered, was kind and naïve. Wife material. Tailor-made for the long, long, ever-after that could have been. It was impossible to get through even part of the day without Tanya's image appearing. It played over and over in his mind like a favorite video. Brad tortured himself by preserving these memories, tenacious in his effort to keep them from fading. With renewed promise to himself, Brad vowed to give his self-esteem a major overhaul. He would start by turning to his backup love—the love of skiing. He could always count on the slopes to assuage his trampled feelings and to hold out new hope. Now, to set his plan in motion!

Early the next morning, Brad began the task of rearranging business appointments. He hurriedly filled shipping orders and, by altering his schedule, was able to choose the week after next as his departure date. Of course, his destination would be Mt. Stowe. He fixated on the peace that the familiar slopes would provide. He loved the days of serpentine trails and the nights filled with camaraderie and good fun. He welcomed nights that promised to be noisy and busy, rather than nights reverberating with ghosts of the past and the minutia that accompanies a love gone wrong.

The first morning at the familiar chalet, Brad stood on the balcony, inhaling deeply. His lungs expanded as he hungrily sucked in the soothing air and the familiarity all around him. He felt like a long-lost stranger who had come home at last. The wondrous iridescence of the pale white slopes called to him, beckoning him to take comfort as the frisky wisps of wind buffeted the banks of freshly fallen snow. But the exhilaration was short-lived as through the glitter of the snowflakes, another image persistently pushed itself to the foreground. Tanya was back once more. Brad visualized her eyes, eyes enlivened with a curiosity which had been so sadly lacking in the early stage of their ill-fated love affair. Yet again he recalled the numerous times he had tentatively tried to address their mutual problem. But no go. It simply wasn't to be. He found the mere thought upsetting.

Brad headed for the t-bar, involuntarily clutching his poles. He was suddenly a man of steel and his magnetic properties were by now an extension of his thoughts—a magnetic tangible link to happier times. He welcomed the slaloms which gave him a compelling reason to focus, a reason to offset failure. Every win was a 'thank you' to him self. Thanks for proving his self-worth. Three weeks, two days, and seven long hours had passed since Tanya had crushed his attempt to talk things out. His life was a shambles, much worse since his heart-breaking experience at the computer workshop in Florida. Brad coped by taking a handful of days at a time, seeking solace from the solitary sport of skiing. With each day of skiing over, as well as the après-ski cocktails and dinner, Brad found himself taking orders from his emotions rather than his common sense. This caused no end of private pain.

In his narrow cot, late into the night, jumbles of thoughts often came unbidden. But tonight there was a diversion from Brad's 'Tanya' thoughts. Tonight it was raven-haired Mitch who loomed as large as a seriously solitaire-ed trophy. The Mitch, who could kiss and bite concurrently. The Mitch, who reminded him of their past cyclonic embraces. The Mitch, who was exciting and baggage-free. Dear Mitch with her toolbox crammed full of woman perks. She had indeed been a godsend to his battered ego left in Tanya's wake. True, Mitch had been second choice, but also a welcome available option. Right at this very moment, he wished she were here. Brad wallowed in the memory of the exhilaration and exuberance that only she could emit. As a result of the soul-baring talks, late into the nights, he knew that Mitch would run like the wind from love and marriage. She openly admitted her aversion to commitment. Men had expected far too much from her and these experiences had been disappointing, all too often turning her world a dull isolated grey.

Brad and Mitch had been lucky to have found solace in each other. They had trusted in each other's ability to avoid commitment while elevating their outlet for sex. Sex seemed to be that ubiquitous excuse for most people and they were no different. Both males and females, dating back to Adam and Eve, had paved the way to happiness with concrete blocks of sex. Ever since the night that Mitch had tilted her head and winked at Brad, her signal had become a preliminary step to sexual satisfaction. In her world, she approached men much as an alcoholic approaches booze. One man was one too many and a thousand not enough. Neither diffidence nor forwardness were lost on Mitch as she gobbled up the weeks of her life, trying in vain to fill the void left by the untimely death of her husband— her one all-time perfect love. Brad's thoughts rambled through the past, visualizing Mitch with her provocative wardrobe and her devil-may-care attitude. He recalled the aura that she so successfully emitted, one that could overpower any man or any situation that might arise. She lived for the moment, squeezing life dry, as she went along her way. She did not torture herself with long-term plans or dreams that might not end. To her, dreams were just dreams, all too transitory and disappointing

Since being solidly forced out of Tanya's life, vague parts of long-ago dreams were all that Brad had left. Tanya was like malaria, hanging on in the recesses of his mind. Every time he thought he had her beaten she would sneak back, recurring time after inappropriate time. Maybe Mitch would be the antibiotic for curing him once and for all. Or would the avoidance of women altogether be the only hope in hell he had?

Brad tossed and turned and wrestled with his demons but he couldn't get the upper hand of things. How does one fire his emotions, or at the very least, demote them to a manageable level? Realizing that he could not escape the ravages of love forever, Brad set out to plan escape routes and alternatives. Once again he fell back on his desire to improve his skiing ability. He would be the very best he possibly could be. Better was not good enough. He needed to be all-consumed, so much so, that he could blot out the horizontal hulas and the wayward waltzes that had held him and Mitch together on the dance floor of their short relationship. He thought back on his repeated attempts to reach Mitch, but they had proven as fruitless as his attempts to talk things out with Tanya.

Brad finally fell into a fitful sleep with dissonant images of love traipsing through his dreams. He pictured Mitch, angry and consumed by his sudden unexplained departure. She would once again consider herself a woman duped. At best she would create havoc with herself, further vowing to turn male intention up-side-down. Little did she know that, that was exactly what she had done. Nothing Mitch did fell into the predictable category because she herself didn't know from one minute to the next how she might handle any given situation. In his dreams, Brad saw her eyes. Beautiful emerald eyes filled with mistrust, yet sometime promise. Because of his unexplained departure, Brad knew he would fall into the 'mistrust' category. And her look of scorn would be forever tattooed on his conscience.

CHAPTER SIXTEEN

Tanya was consumed by her desire to come to terms with her shattered love life. There must be a way to get past the hurt. Brad's infantile behavior concerning the sending of the hurtful fax, stuck in her mind like a burr. It would not go away. Despite her determination to develop a new focus, she found it difficult to fill the empty spaces of her day-to-day existence. The biggest space of all was the vacancy left by her separation from Brad. Another void, although not so troublesome, concerned Sven. Contact him, or not? That was the question. The indecision was draining and counterproductive, as far as getting down to business was concerned. Many days at the office were spent burying her emotions under the blanket of mundane details such as answering the phone, filing, carding, and so forth.

In her bewilderment, Tanya seesawed from missing Brad to possibly contacting Sven. She was not yet home-free as far as Sven was concerned. She had not forgotten, but she was determined not to be drawn back into his addictive web. Sven, lover of women . . . man of counterfeit smile . . . body of a god.

Maybe it was just pure fate, a fate set in motion by her devastating loss of love. A rebound situation! Whatever it was, it had allowed her to be entrapped in the dynamics of Sven's sexual equation. Tanya admitted that the passivity of Brad's antiseptic love had not prepared her for the raw lust that Sven had offered. She sorely missed the special feeling that Sven had unleashed, but she became angry every time she thought about the irresistible appeal that his ability to take control had created. It also angered her that she had put Sven's needs first, while allowing hers to settle for a distant second. She chastised herself over and over again, and it was during one of these self-tormenting sessions that Tanya struck upon an idea. She would take up skiing! Seriously try to infiltrate Brad's world. See why he was so enamored by it all. This would also enable her to put additional space between herself and Sven. Get him out of her mind once and for all.

There was no one more surprised than Tanya's boss on Monday morning when she marched into his office and requested a two-week holiday in mid-January. The girl who hated winter! What an about turn. She was the girl who had been adamant in chasing sunshine and blue skies. Tanya ran over her plans again in her mind. She was relieved that she already had ski togs, equipment, and of course, the basic nuances of skiing that Brad had earlier foisted upon her. All of this saved time. Now all she had to do was get right down to the business of honing her very ordinary skills. As a result of her time spent with Sven, Tanya had become rather calculating and forward. Now she was not above packing her toolbox with new ideas and woman perks, ready to pull them out and use them at an opportune time.

The ski lodge that Tanya chose was small but adequate, quaint but unpretentious. Her choice was based on the fact that superior ski instructors could be found there in January. This fact was soon borne out, as Tanya found herself bone-tired each night, as a result of the rigid demands of her instructor and the challenge of the ski trails. It took everything she had some days just to hang in and she found herself questioning the wisdom of her decision to take up skiing in the first place. In the long run, she knew that even the fatigue, as bad as it could be on some days, could not compare to the draining possibility of never seeing Brad again.

After sweating and straining through the first week of intensive training, Tanya found herself steeped in a brand new awareness. This new feeling was good. She was captured by the splendor all around her. The little spurts of swirling snow, so annoying before, now felt surprisingly good. How had she been blind for so long? Each morning had a special-ness. She was awake well in advance of the errant rays of weak sunshine that broke through the very early dawn. Normally, Tanya was not a morning person but now all that had changed. Now she rushed through her toilet and breakfast eager to be amongst the first of early avid skiers.

Tanya appreciated even the feeblest of sun rays which were magnified by the glitter of the freshly fallen snow. Never before had she beheld such a beautiful scene. She didn't want to miss even a little bit of it. She shivered, not from the cold, but from the wonder all around her as she hurried toward the starting point. As she raced down the mountain, exuberant flumes of snow marked her confident twists and turns. Her instructor smiled proudly as he watched her close in on the challenge of the final decent. "That girl", he thought, "was born to be a winner". Tanya was also buoyant, filled with self-satisfaction. She couldn't help feeling both daunted and pleased by her performance in the awesome world of skiing.

Tanya's high didn't end when she propped her skis up alongside so many others that evening, for now she became part of the commaradie of the après-ski group in which acquaintances became fast friends. And she knew best friends often became lovers. And lovers all too often became arbitrators in the sexual arena. But friends, lovers, or arbitrators all shared a common love of the slopes. This magic seemed exclusively available to all skiers as the comings and goings of the trainers and their students spelled excitement. One felt a special belongingness that nothing else could equal. This is what Brad must have felt. This is what he had tried so hard to get across to her. At long last, Tanya finally understood.

On the slopes again, Tanya's instructor was relentless as he pushed her to the limit. Her final four days interpreted into a torturous regime. She ached to be the very best in the class, not wanting to disappoint either her coach or herself. Days were filled with rigorous practice, while evenings were filled up with shopping for the perfect new ski outfit. Tanya had a plan and that plan called for her to look her very best. It was not until the very last evening, prior to flying home, that Tanya stumbled upon the perfect ensemble. It was proudly displayed in the most unlikely place in the tiny skiing village, tucked into the end unit of an exclusive enclave. A perfect Bogner number! It was glitzy topaz, tasteful without being gauche. Pale mink collar and cuffs complimented the unique jacket. The design was superb, especially for Tanya, in that it had a cleverly tapered waistline which tended to slenderize the wearer. And it was plain. No buckles. No drawstring. No added trim. Tanya tried it on, turning this way and that. She studied herself from every angle. No! It wasn't her imagination. The outfit did make her look taller. And the matching earmuffs complimented her sun-streaked hair. The head to toe effect was dazzling! Now, to initiate the rest of her plan. Her plan was designed with built-in damage control to offset the sorry biography of the last week that she and Brad had spent together.

Despite fatigue brought on by days of intensive training and the pending flight home, the time to lovingly hang up her precious outfit and to arrange her toiletries before falling into bed. Tomorrow she would get right down to business. Put the final touches on her devious plan. She fell asleep with wording and rewordings tumbling through her brain. She daren't slip up. This chance might never pass her way again. After wording and rewording her message, at least a dozen times, the following morning Tanya was finally ready to send the most important message of her life. It read: Hi Brad. Place: Mt. Stowe Chalet. Time: 7:30 pm, Feb. 14th. Purpose: Re-kindle old flame. And, yes, her message was going via fax! Touche! It was no mistake that she had chosen Valentine's Day for the surprise liaison in Vermont. She needed all the help she could get and she was counting on cupid to see her through.

Tanya hurried to the fax machine as quickly as possible in case she might lose her nerve or change her mind. Her hands trembled and her mind raced as she prepared to send off the fax of her lifetime. She had extended her winter holiday and would hopefully meet Brad in two day's time. If everything came off as planned, that is. The politics of her decision still bothered her but the probable thrill of seeing Brad once more had won out.

Thoughts of Sven were being eliminated slowly but surely. One day at a time. Soon Tanya hoped to reach the point of excluding Sven altogether. She couldn't just sit back and wait for Brad to call. That might never happen and she refused to allow herself to think about any scenarios with endings not to her liking. She now knew what she wanted. Brad's absence, even for a day, became an aching void. Her actions were well thought out. This was no rush to judgment, but instead, a last-ditch effort to bring Brad and her life into line.

CHAPTER SEVENTEEN

Dawn heralded a day which promised to be bright and sunny. This kind of day had a crispness that naturally elevated one's spirits and Brad was no exception. As usual, he was one of the first to rise. He whistled his way through a quick shower and stepped out onto the balcony to breathe in the fresh cold air of the morning. He felt a private relationship to the spectacular sunrise before him. He and the universe were in sync as a silent energy pulsated around him. He had not felt this good in a long, long time. He sucked in one long last breath of special-ness, before stepping inside and shutting the door.

There was a lilt in Brad's step as he made his way to the cafeteria. Only one other fellow skier had already appeared, but before Brad could acknowledge him, or even have a quick sip of coffee, he was summoned to the small antique office of the ski lodge. It almost felt like déjà vu. When he stepped through the door, he was handed a fax. As Brad read the terse message, his heart began to beat rapidly. He read the words—"Hi Brad!"

Place: Mt. Stowe Chalet. Time: Feb. 14th, 7:30 pm. Purpose: Rekindle old flame. Mitch! he thought. It was so like something she'd do. And on Valentine's Day! A special day for special lovers! Just like her to concoct a spur-of-the-moment reunion. Try to throw him off balance. Surprise him. An eager smile lit up Brad's face. The very thought of Mitch played havoc with his hormones. Maybe for a short time he would be able to re-route his misery by putting the ghost of Tanya out of his mind.

Back in the cafeteria again, Brad grinned like a schoolboy in between gulps of his cooled-down coffee. A sinuous carelessness overtook him and now he was more anxious than ever to hit the slopes, gobble up the day, and get closer to the appointed time of 7:30 pm. A twinge of mild torment consumed him as his thoughts turned to Tanya. God! How he wished things could have been better. He wondered where Tanya was and what she might be doing this very minute. He was prepared to forgive her in a heartbeat, even accept her on her own terms. He'd even let her lead the way. He'd follow and be more than happy to have a second chance. He'd be happy even to be a subplot in her overall plan.

Brad's day was wonderful even if rift with impatience. It promised to be unique as no other had ever been. It was just a feeling of anticipation that had almost completely overtaken him and he could hardly wait for evening. The meandering ski trails took on a specific appeal as Brad effortlessly took on challenge after challenge. Being a creature of nature, as well as a creature of habit, Brad welcomed the glistening snow crystals which accompanied each playful gust of wind. It was the early morning fax that had reshaped his whole day, giving it a lift, a new prospective. In fact as the day progressed, Brad had to force himself not to leave the slopes early. This feeling was a first for him. He wanted to have time to prepare himself for the onslaught of potent femininity that Mitch so naturally exuded. He would order champagne and an intimate dinner for two.

Brad had never forgotten how Mitch had assailed his sexuality, drawing to the surface sensations that he never knew he had. But through it all, he had always felt a little out of his element with her, in over his head so to speak. But he promised himself that tonight would be different.

In a small town, two hours away by plane, Tanya had been up since the crack of dawn, too excited to waste time in bed. She pampered herself with a long luxurious bath. She lovingly rubbed lotion over her lithe new body and her newly-manicured nails. She had even managed to squeeze in a pedicure the day before. Her hair shone from a fresh shampoo of the latest herbal ingredients. Love makes things more acute and accurate, and so Tanya's enthusiasm achieved a sharper edge. This edge continued to escalate right up to the very minute that Tanya's plane touched down and as she boarded the shuttle bus for the lengthy ride to the foyer of the ski lodge.

Tanya looked good and she knew it. Her anticipation had conquered, then stilled, the turmoil of the time spent with Sven in Florida. Any previous expected permanency with him had quietly died. Now it would be Brad's job to keep the ghosts at bay. Tanya had done much soul-searching concerning her self, as well as Brad, before deciding that Brad was the only one who could supply the missing link to a long and lasting relationship. She and her self were at one as far as her future was concerned

Tanya's timing was perfect. Determined to demonstrate her new sense of self and her special distinction, she strategically placed herself just inside the door of the Bristo. She felt nervous and shaky, and her mouth was as dry as new cotton. She quivered as she waited. To hide the trembling of her hand, she tucked it into the pocket of her glitzy topaz outfit. Her other hand held firm, clutching her barely-used skis. Her attempt at nonchalance was painfully obvious and her flushed face was a dead giveaway. Even to casual observers, she was exceptionally ill at ease.

Tanya noticed Brad as soon as he entered the room. She watched him as he cautiously scanned the room, his bulky sweater moving through a sea of bulky sweaters much like his own. The suspense was unbearable as she awaited his reaction. She had never before taken a chance like this. What on earth had she been thinking? Brad was almost to the bar before he caught a glimpse of her. He momentarily froze, before getting his bearings and refocusing upon her. It had dawned on him! He was staring at the sender of the fax!

Cautiously, Brad took a tentative step forward, before they rushed into the waiting arms of each other.

"You've changed", Brad simply stated.

"You mean my wardrobe?" Tanya asked, caressing the sleeve of her shiny new jacket.

"That too!" Brad replied, "but it's more than that."

"You haven't. You're exactly the same loving guy that I left so long ago."

Brad looked solemn as he whispered, "I have decided that I won't either. At least, as far as you and I are concerned."

"Shall I help you with your bags, honey?"

"Thanks! I booked #14."

CHAPTER EIGHTEEN

Grasping Tanya's bags firmly, Brad led the way toward her room. No sooner had they rounded the corner in the dimly lit hall, than Brad set the bags down and reached to pull Tanya close to him. His mouth worked in perfect harmony with his adventurous hands, while Tanya's arms did their part by crushing him even closer. This was so new to them. So was each embrace that was unwittingly turning into preparatory foreplay, so essential to their personal crescendo. Brad blazed a trail of hot tiny kisses over Tanya's ear, down her neck, only coming to a standstill when he reached her firm breasts.

Gone was Tanya's carefully planned strategy as she wondered how much longer she could hold on before dragging Brad to the floor or the wall or the bed, whichever came first. She couldn't understand herself. She had never felt this way before. Nor had she ever felt so hot. Not even with Sven and the backdrop of a sultry Florida night. But down deep, she knew that it was that Floridian experience that she intended to put to use this very night. Brad's restraint was slowly but surely being undermined as penis and heart pounded in perfect orchestra.

The slam of a door farther down the hall abruptly brought them to their senses, and Brad sheepishly reached for the bags, eager to cover the short distance to Room #14. Tonight he intended to give Tanya a night like she'd never know before, for, he too, had experiences that begged to be put into service.

Barely inside the room, Brad dropped the bags again as he and Tanya lunged at each other. Heat smoldered through Tanya's Bogner slacks, a special heat emanating from the brief lace panties that barely concealed her womanhood. Brad, fired by this long awaited contact, groaned as he hooked his thumb in the elasticized waistband of Tanya's slacks, while his other thumb attempted to jockey the restraining pants down over her shapely hips. His left hand cupped her buttocks, as he urged her forward while simultaneously tilting her pelvis upward. Or was this maneuver Tanya's doing? It didn't really matter for they strove toward a mutual goal. Brad's eyes bored into the eyes of the woman he adored as his tongue slid into her mouth with a probing intensity.

He managed to maintain eye contact as he ran his hand up the inside of her thigh, caressing the silken highway as he went. Gently but firmly, he shoved his middle finger deep inside her. She shivered like an aspen leaf as his index finger also found its way. Never before would Brad have dared to venture this far. Nor would Tanya have permitted it. But experience had removed the adolescent barriers and now the time for adult love had come.

Familiar heat permeated Tanya's groin as she came to terms with the true meaning of unrestrained lust. But was she finally ready to deal with this undiluted passion that Brad was holding out? This was no time for silly indecision. That part of her life was over and she had laid all misgivings to rest. Her indecision was pushed aside by Brad's kisses and rhythmic foreplay, intensifying as it catapulted them both to a stage of readiness. They had never been this far before but Brad wanted to savour this precious moment. He wanted their first time to be memorable and perfect rather than jut an animalistic rut. It took superhuman effort to slowly withdraw his fingers out and upward parting the folds as he caressed her pouting clitoris. Reluctantly he tugged Tanya's slacks up and pulled her to her feet.

"Let's have a celebratory drink. We've found each other at last". Brad motioned toward the tiny bar where a bottle of chilled champagne awaited. "I'll slip into something comfortable" offered Tanya as she headed for the bathroom that also doubled as a dressing room. Immediately she began the 'preen' of her lifetime. She just had to look good. No, she had to look her very best.

As far as Brad was concerned, Tanya took too long and he found himself once more becoming impatient to move things right along. But he had to admit it was worth the wait when she appeared clad in amber coloured lounging pyjamas which complimented her tawny skin and golden hair. Brad noticed every detail as he scrutinized the beautiful woman before him. He took in the neckline of the semi-sheer top that barely concealed protruding nipples. Brad also appreciated the matching pants which were the only thing covering her firm behind.

"To us!" Brad toasted, as he held high his long stemmed glass. The gentle clink of crystal was response enough. Tanya was too emotional to speak. The mood was set. Everything was tailor-made for a night of long awaited love. Brad's hard body and rigid penis just hoped they'd make it through the romantic candle light dinner without exploding. The flowers, the candlelight, and the food were complimented by soft music in the background. Brad and Tanya nibbled the food but devoured each other.

Coffee and liquors seemed to take forever and it had come to the point in time where Brad had completely run out of restraint. He could contain himself no longer. He needed release and he hoped Tanya did too. Carefully he set his glass aside and was relieved to see Tanya follow suit. Ever so slowly he pulled Tanya to her feet and after a tantalizing full-body embrace, crab walked her to the bed.

Eagerly, they undressed each other before sinking as one to the lumpy narrow cot. Tanya's warm breasts pillowed against Brad's hairy chest as he pressed into her. They kissed hungrily as Brad's fingers once more sought out the coveted moist triangle. As he slid his fingers into the familiar crease, moist turned to wet and Tanya's legs developed a will of their own. In one fluid motion, her legs parted wide as she turned to straddle Brad. Her hand quivered as she stroked his upright sheath. Her thumb traced tiny circles on the broad tip as she put into play her recently acquired skills. At last they were ready to do what they should have done a long time ago.

Again positions were reversed as Brad assumed the top position and bent his head in search of lip and nipples. His passion by now was rising in lightning crests, threatening to turn him into a sexual inferno. Tanya's body language signified complete readiness starting with her pouting nipples, past her highly held buttocks, and ending at the inviting furnace between her legs. As Brad prepared to mount her, both he and she croaked an 'I love you". Sweet fire raged but only for a short time before each felt the other's shudder of release. Sooner than either thought possible, again Brad and Tanya coupled, only this time Tanya gave new meaning to the missionary position. She became a sexual predator claiming her long-time-in-coming prey.

Later lying on the narrow cot, subdued and satisfied, errant thoughts drifted into unbidden territories as both Brad and Tanya defined what they felt. Their love, like love in general, was exciting. But trust is fragile, and both knew that if the mix was not precisely right, the recipe would fail and be rendered futile. As lovers they had learned their lessons well and both were adamant in not letting ghosts from their time spent apart interfere with their desire to build a life together.

As the lovers lay together in the quietness of each other's thoughts, dreams came unbidden and uninvited. Tanya found herself assaulted by parts of a long ago dream. It came in the form of Sven, haunting and bittersweet, as its ghost played out its final scene. Sven, the mentor who had taught her to approach love as a team sport. Yet it was he who had tired of the game and dropped the ball. Tanya visualized Sven's eyes, eyes emitting such profound sexual energy. His image was fading but it would take much longer still to forget his smooth behaviour. His mode of operation had become a trademark of his daily existence. Business and love were handled alike as far as Sven was concerned.

Brad stirred ever so slightly as, he too, was putting the final touches of farewell to his past. In his reverie he saw Mitch who without fuss or promise had provided a haven for him in his darkest hours following his split with Tanya. If nothing else, Mitch was an undisputed authority on gender difference and what to do about it. It was she who had exposed him to new influences and broadened his horizons. It all seemed vague and long ago as he recalled his time on the slopes with her. Everything had happened so fast and faded so quickly. He had been so broken and vulnerable. But now Mitch was just part of the slopes and the sky and the lustful evenings in the damp romantic lodge. She had come and gone so quickly, like a brief tornado touching down in a time of deep despair.

As Brad and Tanya lay entangled in each other's arms, all memories of Sven and Mitch became 'forever' secrets, transparent ghosts of yesterday. Ultimately choice of love and loyalty had come into play and they had found each other. Both wanted a married life together and they knew that it could only be founded on trust, regardless of their individual definitions of love.

This time Brad and Tanya would be held together by a love that was not only powerful but complete. Transitory though meaningful, their flings of the past, known to each but not by each other, quietly faded and died. The conflicts that had turned their world topsy-turvy were finally settled. Nothing that had come before now mattered. It was light years from the love that they had now begun to build. As their bodies spoke, conversation had no place. There was no room in their new love for empty promises that all too often crisscross the courtship rituals of novice lovers. Love this time would be perfect. They would create an ideal foundation to serve as a platform for their happily-ever-after.

Brad and Tanya were quickly recapturing the impetus that had been so rudely interrupted by the hasty senseless fax. They had come fill circle. The past no longer mattered. All that mattered now was the life they would share together. They lay quietly staring at each other, each holding out a mutual building block for the foundation of perfect love.

Printed in the United States
By Bookmasters